Everywhere I Go

Skylar L. Hill

1

First Edition Published 2018 by Bob Scott Publishing

www.facebook.com/BobScottPublishing

Cover By: Skylar L. Hill

Text Copyright 2017 Skylar L. Hill

Chapter 1

Both my feet were almost out the door before I heard, "Julie, I need you." I am getting sick and tired of my mother yelling at me to do things all the damn time. I can never get away from her. Whenever I try to be social my mother ruins it for me. For the past three years it's been like this: "Julie do this, Julie do that." She also always demands things; she never asks me politely to do things for her. I hate it! Today's conversation was the worst of them all.

"Julie, I need this house spotless. The doctor is coming by tonight since I'm not feeling good."

"Well, maybe if you wouldn't be lying around all the damn time you would feel fine. You never leave the house or your room for that matter. You make me do everything for you."

"Well, I'm sorry you feel this way. I feel like if it wasn't for your father leaving us I wouldn't be this way."

"Don't you dare blame my father for any of this! If it wasn't for you being so demanding my dad would still be around!"

"Julie, you better take all that back right now. I'm not demanding! I don't deserve any of this attitude from you, young lady."

"I don't care anymore! I'm done taking orders from you! You don't treat me like your daughter. You treat me like a slave. I've put up with it long enough. Three years. Not anymore."

After that I ran out of my mother's room and slammed the door. I was so frustrated. I got especially mad when my mother yelled, "You need help. A professional's help for this matter." That's what made me flare up. I didn't need help. I was this way because of her. If she would let me go out of the house more than once a year I wouldn't be this way.

It had gotten to the point where she enrolled me in online classes for school. I don't even get out of the house for groceries. She has a service drop them right off at the door. I was enslaved in my own house. I had no freedom or friends. I hated every moment of my life!

It all started three years ago on a rainy Saturday afternoon. My mom and dad were yelling again when I got back from spending the night with my best friend Alexandria. My mom was yelling at my dad accusing him of being a good old worthless piece of nothing. My mom had in her little mind that my dad was cheating on her with a good friend from work. My dad was an engineer and had to work late nights, which my mother couldn't understand, no matter how much and how hard my dad tried to convince my mother he wasn't cheating, and that his friend only did professional work with him. This friend was also currently married and getting ready to have a kid with her husband. I knew that there was no way my dad could be cheating with this lady friend. My mother couldn't and didn't want to believe him. The arguing continued for the next three days. Then as soon as I walked in the door that Tuesday afternoon after school I heard my mother yell, "Get your stuff out and leave. You have one hour to leave." When I heard that I ran to my room crying. I couldn't believe what I just heard.

I didn't want my dad leaving. I was daddy's little princess. What was I going to do without my dad around. I loved him so much. He was the only one I trusted with everything I went through. Whenever I had a rough day he was the one I ran to. He and I did almost everything together. I cried for a good three hours that day. I refused to eat dinner that night just because I knew it would be impossible for me to face my mom and dad. I could just hear them from my room fighting about every little thing. It didn't matter the subject. Once it got on the topic about who's fault it was that the family was falling apart I threw my favorite chair across the room and knocked a few books off my shelf. I'm surprised that my parents didn't hear it and come rushing up to my room. I guess they were too busy yelling at each other to even notice their daughter. I could be up in my room dying and they wouldn't care. I just didn't understand why they had to play the blame game on each other. It shouldn't be anyone's fault that we are falling apart. We should all just stay together and be a big, happy, and loving family.

Several questions ran through my head that night. I couldn't understand why my parents were doing this. I didn't know if it was my fault. I didn't know how my life would change. I just kept asking myself these things. Then right before bed that night, my dad came in my room to tuck me in.

"Hey, princess. Are you okay? I know this is hard for you. This is really difficult for me as well. It's a stressful situation. I don't understand why your mom is acting like this. She knew that before I even took this job that I would be working a lot of late nights. We had a discussion about this before I signed the contract agreeing that I would take the job. We sat at the table together, read over the contract, and she saw me sign it, She is blowing everything out of proportion. She is ridiculous. I can tell you one thing for sure is that whatever does end up happening will be just fine. I will always remember you and love you. Please don't ever forget that."

"I won't, Dad. I promise. I will be okay about this whole situation though, Dad. The one thing I just don't understand is why you and mom can't get along better. I thought you guys loved each other. You guys obviously loved each other enough to get married. Can't you guys just re-spark what you guys once had? I don't want you guys to get a divorce and you leave. Mom won't even let me chose who I want to live with. If I was able to chose I would make sure that I go with you. I don't want to stay here with my mother. I can guarantee you that she would make my life a terrible nightmare. "

"I know, sweetie. I still love your mother. My feelings for her will never change, but it looks like she doesn't feel the same way about me anymore. I wish there was still chemistry between us. There just isn't anymore. I doubt that there will ever be sparks between us again. I hope you can understand all of this. You may hurt for a while, but you will be just fine without me. All I want you to do is listen to you mother. That is the best thing for you right now. Just please understand that I don't want to leave you either. I wish I could take you with me but your mother just won't let me. You are a fight that I won't win no matter how hard and how much I fight. I can promise you that I will see you again. So just think of it this way. It isn't goodbye, it's just a see you later. I will always love you. Nothing will ever change that."

After my dad said that he gave me a good night's kiss and we hugged for a couple minutes. I didn't want to let go, but I knew that I had to try and get some sleep. I had school the next morning. I wish I didn't though. I did have the thought about sneaking into my dad's car at night when he wasn't looking so if he did take off I would be right there with him. The more I thought about it I didn't want it all to backfire on him if he were to get caught with me. Knowing my mom she would tell cops that my dad kidnapped me and he would most likely end up in jail. I definitely didn't want that to happen. I wouldn't be able to see my dad if that event occurred. I decided to listen to my dad and just stay with my mom no matter how much I didn't want to. It truly was going to kill me inside.

When I got up the next morning I got ready for school just like any other day, even though I didn't want to go to school that day. I knew something was different because I didn't smell breakfast cooking or anything like I usually do. My mother always cooks breakfast for me no matter what. When I got downstairs I went past my parents room, all of my dad's stuff was gone. I ran out to the garage and my dad's car was gone. So I knew at that moment that it was done. My parents weren't together anymore. It broke my heart to even think about that. The thought made my mind go off of not having breakfast. When I went to school that day my dad was the only one on my mind. I even broke into tears once or twice throughout the day. I had to sit in the principal's office because apparently I was distracting everyone in my class. I could understand that. It was just hard for me. Especially since I didn't get to say goodbye to my dad the morning before he left.

That was what broke my heart the most. I thought that he would have a little bit more decency to come and at least tell me good bye. I didn't even want to get on the bus to go home. I just wanted to stay at the school or at least somewhere that wasn't home. I knew that when I got home that things would be completely different. I wasn't ready for change. The minute that I stepped in the front door my life definitely did change. It was completely different.

Chapter 2

My mother had a huge attitude change. Three years later and nothing has changed. I've even tried sneaking out of the house at night when she was sleeping. That hasn't came close to working. Apparently, she somehow had a security lock installed when I didn't know. Now each time I try to sneak out there is a loud siren that goes off and will wake my mother up. It truly sucks. I was not lucky in any of my attempts to escape. It was like my mother wanted to hold me like a prisoner in my own house for the rest of my life. I was confined with nothing fun to do. I just wanted to have a normal life like the rest of the teenagers I knew. I wanted to make the same mistakes that everyone had the chance to make. I wanted to go to parties and have a great time with friends. My mother made that impossible.

It got to the point where I have even tried to get a hold of my dad to see if he would come and rescue me from this place I call home. I have tried every day with no success. I have finally decided to do something I know I'll probably regret later, but I was tired living the way I was and I wanted to find my dad. I didn't want to continue dealing with my mother and her stupid depression. I knew it was something she really couldn't control, but she could control if she got out of her bed and did things.

I could understand as well why she was this way. When she was sixteen years old my mom's sister died of cancer. I think that is one thing that took a big toll on the whole family. A year later my mom's dad left her and her mom. With my mom's dad leaving her and her mom is why when she was nineteen years old my mom met my dad and they got married. Three years later my parents had me. The first twelve years after I was born were the happiest years for me. My parents actually loved each other and would do things with me. There was one night though that changed the life of my parents and I.

One night my parents were invited to go to a party. They decided that it would be a good opportunity to go out for a night. I was staying over at a friend's. I had so much fun with her. We stayed up all night because we ate a lot of candy right before we went to bed. We then told ghost stories before we tried to go to sleep and so I was too scared to go to sleep. My parents decided to get me that night before the morning. I tried to convince them to let me stay until the morning but I didn't win that fight. When I got home things went from bad to worse.

Right when I stepped into the house my mom pushed me down. I didn't think she meant to but then when I got back up she just pushed me back down. These outbursts kept happening for the next three months. When I finally did tell someone the only thing that happened was I was taken out of the house until my mother did an alcohol and abuse prevention program. After she finished that I was right back in that house. I missed my mom when she was happy and would actually do things with me.

Maybe if I found my dad he would make sure that I had the life that I deserved to have. I missed him so much and wanted things to go back to the way they were two years ago.

So one day after I did my classes for the day I went into my room and packed a bag. I only packed a few outfits, my laptop, my phone, electronics, a book, a charger, food, water, some money, and a sleeping bag. Then that night when my mom was sleeping I would just run for it. I didn't care if the alarm went off or not. I didn't want to be in this house any longer than I have already. It wasn't fair that I couldn't be a kid. I needed a life that was healthy for me and my mom. If I stayed at the house any longer my mom would just get worse and depend on me a lot more. That wasn't healthy for her. So in my thinking this would be in the best interest for both me and her. She may not think so, but I knew that it would be. If my plan worked the way that I wanted to then I would be lucky enough that I would already be out to the street and be on my way by the time my mother yelled for me. I knew she wouldn't get off her butt to chase after me. If she did care about me that is what she would do, but she didn't care about me. That was the huge difference about those thoughts. I knew exactly what she would do if she even cared to do anything. She would call the police, they would come out to the house and start to search for me, but by then I would hopefully be miles away. I couldn't wait for my adventure to begin.

So then around ten I tiptoed out of my room down the hall to my mother's room. In my opinion I was like a mouse wanting to get across the floor to get some food without anyone seeing me and trying to kill me. I made sure that I had my slippers on as well. I quietly opened her door just a little to make sure that she was sleeping and to make sure that I didn't wake her up. When I knew for sure that she was asleep I grabbed my bag and went to the door. I was feeling so many emotions. I was happy that I was taking a risk, but I was also feeling nervous. I also had really bad anxiety. The thought of me getting caught kept running through my head. I could get in trouble with not only my evil mother but with the police as well. Then on the other hand if the police caught me maybe they would figure out that my mother treats me the way that she does, and they would make sure that I was placed somewhere where I would be safe and wouldn't be treated the way that I am now. That was definitely a risk I wanted to take.

I knew that the alarm doesn't go off until you put a foot out. I counted to three and made my move. As usual, the alarm went off. I didn't hear my mother yell which was unusual, but I was finally free. I ran as far as my legs could take me. Maybe my mother losing control of her actions and not trying to fix them was a sign that she didn't care, and finally realized that the way she has been treating me was wrong. I knew that what I was doing was the right thing for me.

After running for twenty minutes I stopped. I thought to myself I'm far enough away from that torturous place that they won't be able to find me, at least for tonight anyways. I then decided to go and try to search for my dad. I had no idea where to start.

I then thought that last time I knew my dad worked for a contractor about a few hours away. That was the first place he would be. It was going to take me all night. I started walking. I knew the address of the place but I didn't know the phone number. I wish I did though so i could just call and see if my dad was there. I didn't know the name of it either I just knew what it looked like and where it was located. I started walking. I knew from the beginning that it was going to be a long and rough night.

It was a cold and dreary night. It was the middle of November. The air was quiet. Definitely something that I wasn't used to. In my mind, I was still waiting for that evil mother of mine to yell my name and demand something from me. I just still couldn't believe my risky plan worked and I actually escaped. Hopefully now I can just stay hidden well enough that if the police were looking for me, which I doubt, but even if they were they wouldn't be able to find me.

The night got colder as it continued. The only noises I could hear were the wind blowing in my face and my own footsteps. It got so cold that I could see my own breath. I had to imagine it was getting close to about midnight. The only reason for my thought is because all the late night cafes were closing. I loved the one cafe but that is just because it reminded me of my dad. He would every once in a while take me to this karaoke cafe and let me sing one or two songs. Most of the time I wrote my own songs and performed them. When I was about five or six I would always mess up, but everyone there would clap for me anyways because I had the courage at that young age to get up in front of people and show them my talent. I got better at performing as I got older. There was also another time where the owner of the cafe was having a little girl's birthday party there and he asked me to perform there for the party. I had to agree. I loved performing in front of people. I had some great times there with my dad.

After my dad left though I never even looked at that place again until now. There was a huge crowd of people coming out of there. I knew that I had to try and hide from the people that were coming out so nobody wondered why a teenage girl like me was out so late. Especially if the owner found me. She would make sure that I found my way back to my mother's. Her and my mother used to be really close friends. That is one thing that I didn't like about the owner. If I ever acted up at the cafe or did something that I knew I shouldn't have been doing she would make sure to go to my mother and my mother would make sure to tell my dad. Even though I was more scared of my mother then I was of my dad, my dad would yell at me loudly if he wanted to. It rarely happened but that is just because in his eyes I could never do anything wrong. He did understand that I do make mistakes but they could easily be changed.

The only problem with me being right there in front of the cafe was that there was nowhere for me to go. There was only one direction and that was straight. I took the risk and ran for it. I had to go find some place that was safe but still hidden well enough that people wouldn't be able to find me. I still had about another ten miles to go. I knew that I should probably find some shelter for the night so I wasn't completely tired for the rest of my journey. If I did find my dad I didn't want to look like a messy child of his and potentially embarrass him. I did not want that to happen so I decided that it was best if I slept tonight.

I did find what looked liked an old abandoned park that no one played on or even came near. It didn't even look like a safe place but I wanted to sleep. I honestly at this point didn't care what happened. My mental health was more important than anything right now. So when I reached the park I climbed into this little tunnel that it had and got my bed all set up. My sleeping bag wouldn't stay flat. It would want to curl up on me and make it difficult to get into it. I was half tempted to just say screw it and just lay on the hard plastic of the tunnel. I kept at it though because I knew it would be safer to lay in the sleeping bag than if I didn't. Since it was in the middle of November there was a good chance that the weather could get below zero. It could even start snowing if it got cold enough to. I didn't want snow at all. Snow was not my best friend. I always get sick when it starts to get colder and starts to snow. I didn't pack any medicine or anything to help me if I did get sick on this adventure. That probably would have been the smart thing to do, but I wasn't thinking at the time of my escape. I just wanted to get away from my mother. The only other thing that I didn't like about where I was sleeping was it wasn't the most comfortable place, but it would work for me. I just wanted a place to get some shut eye. It was dry and hidden.

I surprisingly did get a good night's sleep. I set my alarm to wake me up at six in the morning so I could get a good head start before a lot of people started to head to work.

I did get a good hour walk in before it started to pour down rain on me. I ran to try and find somewhere I could go and stay until the rain had either stopped or slowed down at least. Half of me though just wanted to stay in the rain. I enjoyed feeling the rain come down on me. It gave me a feeling a peace and calmness. That is one thing that my mother and I had in common. We both liked the rain. We would sometimes sit on a back patio and just sit to listen and watch the rain. Those were the only moments that my mother wasn't mean to me. I wish we had more times like that, but I wasn't going to get my way. She had a window in her room and she didn't have to get up from her bed to open it. So I knew that right about now if she wasn't sleeping she had the window open enjoying the rain. Even though the rain did help me I wanted to find a place to stay so I couldn't get soaked.

I then remembered that there was a nice little restaurant less than a mile down the road. My dad used to take me to it all the time. That was the place that we would go if I got good grades in school. Since I loved it there that was my motivation to do my very best in school. I always got straight A's. My dad was and will always be proud of me. I just know it. I ran there. I made it there in about five minutes. I forgot that I had five dollars in my pocket. So I decided to order my favorite lemonade. It was a strawberry with a tad of lime in it. It was also sweet as well as sour. One sip it could be sweet but then the next it would be sour. I never knew when I got it. That is what made it such an amazing drink.

Before I had the chance to order I heard, "Julie, is that you?"

18

I looked behind me and it was my dad's friend Jonathan. I ran up to him and I about knocked Jonathan over. He was six feet tall, he had black hair with pretty green eyes. He looked just like his dad who owned the restaurant.

"Hey, Jonathan. How are you?"

"I have been good. How are you? What are you doing in this part of town? I haven't seen you in years."

"I'm good. I'm actually on the search for my dad. Have you seen him?"

"No, I haven't, sweetie. Last time I saw him was right after your mom kicked him out three years ago."

"Oh, okay. Well I'm heading to check the contractor that he was working for last time I knew. I just stopped in to grab a strawberry lemonade and wait for the rain to stop."

"Well, I'll go get that drink for you. It's on the house."

"Thank you so much, Jonathan."

I would have went to go get the drink myself, but I wasn't allowed in the back of the restaurant ever since my incident.

I used to work for them for a little while before there was a bad accident that happened. I was working late one night so I could get my forty hours a week in. I was doing the dishes when I heard a noise. Jonathan was in the dining area cleaning up all of the tables. So I went to go tell him about the noise and he didn't believe me. He thought that I was just tired and needed to finish up so I could go home and sleep. I thought that he was right. So when I went back to finish I heard the noise again. This time I didn't go tell Jonathan. When I was about done I felt someone behind me. They grabbed me and beat me up. Luckily at this time I was taking martial arts, so I beat them up twice as bad. When Jonathan came back to see what was happening he saw the guy laying on the ground passed out. That was when he just sent me home. He didn't want me working there anymore after that incident. He wanted to keep me safe and so that meant that I couldn't work there anymore. I didn't want to stop working there but I knew it was for my safety.

After I received the lemonade the rain had stopped and I wanted to start heading back on the road. I continued my journey. I lived in New York City so the walk wasn't so bad. It was really pretty. The scenery is what kept me entertained throughout my adventure. Some of the shops had their fall decorations out already. I loved just looking through the windows just watching all the store employees change the windows so I could see all the different displays. I loved window shopping as well. Which to me meant looking at things that I wish I could buy, but can never afford by myself. I even saw some shops that I have never seen before. I was never allowed this far out of the town. I don't know why though. It looked like a safe part of the city. It was a lot safer than a lot of the parts of the city.

At about nine that night I saw the building. It was right in front of me, this is what I have spent the past twenty three hours looking for. It was a big black building. I knew it was the right building because it always had this one weird smell to it. So I used the speed I would use to run a race to find my dad's one friend. The friend that my mother thought my dad was cheating on her with. I walked up behind her. I shyly said, "Elizabeth?"

She gets scared and jumps. "Yes? Who are you?"

"My name is Julie Scranton to be exact. I'm Joseph Scranton's daughter."

"Joseph Scranton's daughter?"

"Yes, ma'am."

"That's a name I haven't heard in years."

"What do you mean? Doesn't my dad work here?"

"Not anymore. He quit three years ago, when he divorced your mom. Last time I heard he lived two towns over."

"Oh geez. Okay, well thank you. You don't by any chance have his last known address do you?"

"I do. It's at home though. Here, I'll tell you this, why don't you come home with me tonight and rest. You look tired. Then tomorrow morning I'll give you the address."

"Okay. Thank you so much."

"You're welcome, sweetie."

So that night I went home with Elizabeth. Her house was big but scary. Sorta like an abandoned house type of scary. It was gray and smelly that is for sure. I didn't know why anyone would want to live in this house. I thought by the looks of it people would want to run as far away as they possibly could. This is the reason why I was so glad I was only staying a night.

Chapter 3

So the next morning I got up around nine. Elizabeth wasn't up yet so I quietly read my book that I had and waited for Elizabeth to get up. She got up around nine thirty. I had to quickly get on the road since Elizabeth had to be back at work by ten fifteen. She gave me the address and a banana for breakfast. I wasn't really hungry at the time so I just put the banana in my bag to save it for later. Elizabeth also gave me a map so I could easily track where I was going. By the looks of it the house was about another thirty miles from where I was.

I did still have the money that was supposed to be for my lemonade, so I decided to use that money for a taxi. I knew that it would get me about five miles, but every little part helped. So I waved down a taxi and it took me to the very edge of the town. I really wish it would have taken me further though. The town I was about to enter was a really bad one. I knew it was bad when there were police cars on almost every other street just sitting there, waiting for something bad to happen. There was music blaring that had profanity coming out of every single sentence they said. I really didn't want to go through, but I knew I had to so I could find my dad. I wasn't going to give up.

I knew this was a mistake going through here after just a few minutes I heard, "Get away from me you good old piece of nothing." I turned around and saw a fight break out between two girls and a guy. They were all going at each other's necks. I didn't know if I should keep on walking or go help the girls that were getting beat up and yelled at. At first I decided to keep on going since I didn't want to get in the middle of it. It was none of my business. After a minute of walking and thinking I decided to go back and help the poor girls. I hated seeing them like this so I went to try and break it up. When I got to them I got in the middle of them and yelled, "Stop this right now!" at the top of my lungs. That worked, but only for a short while.

Then the guy yelled, "Who do you think you are? Do you know who we are? This isn't your problem to begin with, so just stay out of it and walk away."

"I know who I am, but I don't think you know who you are. You are right I don't know who you are. I do know that none of you should be yelling and going at each other. There is probably a much better way of handling things."

"Well, I think you should leave and let us do what we were doing before you regret anything."

"Whatever. There isn't anything you can do that I haven't been through already in life."

"Is that what you think? We will just see about that." He came over and punched me in the face, which knocked me onto the ground.

The two girls came running over to make sure that I was okay. The one girl said, "I'm so sorry he did that to you. Do you need anything?"

"No, I'm fine. It's my own damn fault. I should have listened to him and just left when he told me to."

"Here, take this pack of ice and keep it on your eye. You better get out of here while you still can. We will be fine. We have dealt with this plenty of times."

"Okay. Thank you so much. Just please be careful. I hate seeing you girls being beat up and called names by this obnoxious guy."

"We will; we promise. Our names are Tina and Angelina."

"Such pretty names. My name is Julie."

"Bye, Julie. Stay safe," both girls said at the same exact time.

After the whole thing I knew I had to get out of this town and fast. I had to take it slow though because a black eye did form and it was hurting really bad. I could barely open my left eye because it was hurting so much. The ice was only helping a little bit. I wish I had some other medicine to help the swelling go down. With only one working eye I could only see from the right side of me. So I knew I had to relax for a little bit to see if the swelling would go down and I could gain some vision back. If I didn't gain my vision back I didn't know what would happen. I did eventually find a bench that I could sit down at for a few minutes until my pain went down a little.

While I was sitting down I heard all of this yelling and fighting. I thought to myself why would anyone want to live in such a horrible town. I knew I had to quickly get out of this town before it got dark and I had to go to sleep. There was no way I was going to go to sleep in this town knowing I may or may not wake up. It was stressing me out staying in this place. The black eye wasn't helping the situation either. I kept touching it every once in awhile to see if it was getting any better, but I think I was just making it worse. I was in so much pain. Luckily it only took me about two hours to get out of this town and into the next. It would have taken me a lot less time if I wasn't in so much pain. I found a nice patch of grass to sleep on, with a wooden bench on it.

I had to figure out how to make a warm bed out of the bench. I knew I still had my sleeping bag with me, but that only helped a tiny bit. Then I figured if I maybe put a couple of layers of clothes on then it would help me stay warm. It would at least keep me comfortable. The only problem was I kept hearing owls. They wouldn't shut up. I tried even covering my ears so I wouldn't hear them as much. Well, I had no luck with that. It was so weird. I never knew owls to be so annoying and loud. After about an hour in a half I finally fell asleep. I slept until the sunrise. It was so bright and beautiful. So I just sat there watching it for a while. After it was done I decided that it was time to get back on the road.

By this time I was starving. I didn't eat at all the day before. I then remembered that I still had the banana that Elizabeth gave me right before I left. So I took that out and slowly ate it. I wanted to savor every single bite since I didn't know the next time I would be able to eat was.

As I was walking I sensed something strange. It felt like I wasn't the only one walking. When I knew for a fact that I heard someone I quickly turned around, but no one was there. I continued my journey.

You could definitely tell that it was Fall. The leaves were falling as well as changing colors. I loved hearing my feet crunch the leaves. The sound was so peaceful. The only thing was I kept hearing leaves crunch behind me. It made me so nervous and jittery. I kept checking behind me, but every time I did there was no one there.

I checked my map to see if I was close to my destination. According to the map I only had two miles to go. So I continued. Then out of nowhere a piece of paper flew into my hands. It read:

I see you, but you don't see me. The journey you are on is useless. You will never succeed until you ask for help.

I looked all around. I couldn't see anyone. I only saw the leaves that I crunched and the trail I have made. Scared for my life I decided to find a hiding spot. There was a little ditch that was surrounded by leaves. That was a nice place I could hide and maybe get away from whoever was watching me. I spent the rest of my night there.

Chapter 4

The next morning was just as creepy as the night before. I kept sensing that something or someone was following me. I ran to my destination. When I got to the house it looked like no one had lived in it for years. The grass was at least a foot tall. There were trees and branches that were hiding the house. I didn't even know where the front door to the house was. I inspected the house. It had the same smell that Elizabeth's house had. I had no idea what was with this smell, it was everywhere I went.

I finally did find the front door. I knocked on the door and waited. There was no answer. I did see that the door was cracked open a little bit so I just walked in. Boy was my prediction right. There was no way that anyone could possibly be living here. All the furniture was covered in cobwebs. Wherever I walked at in that house there were spiders of all kinds. It looked like the spiders have been growing their population in this house for years. I could only imagine how all of this started. I ran out of that place like there was no tomorrow. My dad was definitely not here.

I had no idea where to look for him next. If he wanted to be found I would have already found him by now, or I would at least have a clue where he was. Then I just decided that it was hopeless and I would never find my dad. It was like my dad didn't even want to be found. He promised me he would come back for me. I don't understand why he broke his promise. Maybe it was because he didn't want to deal with my evil mother. I understand that, but he still could've come back for his little princess. I never would have thought that he would just disappear off the face of the earth. I wanted to be with him and only him. With him I wouldn't be so lonely. I would actually have someone that would understand me and the way that I think. I even thought a couple times about going back home and asking my mother if she knew how to get a hold of my dad. The more I thought about it the more I didn't want to go back to what I thought was home.

Then all of a sudden I heard even more noises behind me. I knew it was just my mind playing games on me though. I didn't know if I wanted to continue on with what I started. I knew I had to though. I have come way too far to just give up now. So I decided to go into the woods that I knew was only like three minutes from where I was.

The woods were a nice place and where I belonged. There was plenty of room for me to explore and it barely had any people in them. Even though there were some small noises and some weird smells it was so much better than what I have been used to. If I was at home I would have to smell my mother's room which had dirty clothes, dishes, and dead flies that she would kill if they landed on her. At that point in time I knew the woods were a much better environment for me. I wanted to go and explore so I could find food and water since I was running low. I couldn't go another day without food or water.

The woods were a beautiful sight to see. The trees had pretty leaves on them. There were flowers that surrounded the trees. The flowers must have just bloomed or at least were in the process of blooming. It smelled like lavender. The smell followed me for about twenty minutes. I finally found a pond. The smell came back. I could understand why as soon as I saw the pond. It had a greenish color, wet sand all around it, glass buried in the sand, and the water was freezing cold. I didn't want the pond to be my only water source, but that looked like it was the only one in the woods. I looked around to see if I could find anything I could transport water in it.

I did find a plastic bottle sitting underneath a tree. It was in perfect condition. If anything it looked like someone just opened the bottle, dumped out whatever was in it and then just sat the bottle beneath the tree. That was strange just because everything in the woods appeared to either be broken or dirty. There were broken beer bottles, broken car windows, pieces of steel, and what looked like to be parts of an old car. This was just the one thing that wasn't like everything else. I grabbed it and filled it all the way up to the top with water.

Then after that I did jump into the pond to try and get somewhat clean. I didn't think that it would happen that much just because the pond looked so filthy. As soon as I jumped in though the coldness on my skin felt so good. Like a new sensation. To my surprise and realization it actually helped me get clean. It took away all the dirt. It was a miraculous thing. Everything that was happening was getting stranger and stranger though. Like the smell went away, some of the things that I saw were broken before I went into the pond weren't broken anymore, lastly there seemed to be a lot more flowers than what there were before. Something was going on and I wanted to find out what it was.

When I got back to where I started I decided to start setting up a little camp site for myself. I needed to start a fire so I could have heat. I remember taking a Survival 101 class a year ago. I still remembered some things from that. As soon as I gathered some sticks and some leaves that I found, I got a fire started. When I knew the fire was okay to let burn I left to go and find some fruit and nuts. The fire would help me keep track of where I was set up and everything. It didn't take me long to find enough things that would last me about a couple of days or so. While I was walking back I could see someone or something near my fire. I started running and yelling, "Get away from my fire!"

I scared the life out of whoever it was. He yelled back, "Don't hurt me, I didn't know that anyone else was in these woods."

"Who are you and what are you doing here?"

"My name is Alexander. Who are you?

"My name is Julie. What are you doing in the woods?

"I could ask you the same thing, Julie. I've been exploring these woods for the past five months. It has only been me and no one else. Now all of a sudden you show up. Why?"

"I came in these woods because I didn't think that anyone lived in these woods. I also wanted to start a new life where no one knew me and I could get away from everything and everyone."

"Well, I hope you know I'm the one that has been following you for the past thirty miles. I was there when you got in the fight. I saw everything. The guy that beat you up was my older brother. I felt so bad for you, but to be completely honest with you he did warn you and you didn't listen."

"I don't need your stupid input. I did what I thought was best for the two girls. Your brother obviously didn't respect or care about them at all. I'm sorry that I have a caring spot in my heart for people that I see are hurting. Now please, if you are anything like your jerk of a brother then just please leave. I want nothing to do with you."

"Well, Julie. I want nothing to do with you either if all you are ever going to do is act like is a jerk. I thought you were a nice girl."

"I am a nice person. The only reason why I'm not now is one, because you scared me. Two, you have a nasty attitude. Three, you come from a very mean family as I can see. Lastly, you don't want anything from me except to spy on me and not do anything."

"I wasn't spying on you. I can help you with what you are trying to do. I just won't help you unless you ask for my help. That is how I work around here. If anyone is going to be leaving it will be you. I was in these woods before you and so these woods are mine."

"I'm not leaving. I have a stable camp site here where I will be living from now on. Now get your ass out of here!"

"Not in a million years."

When he said that I screamed so loudly that I think I truly broke him. He fell to the ground covering his ears and screeching.

"I'm sorry that I hurt your ears. I just don't like not getting my way. Now if you will please just go to another section of the woods I would greatly appreciate that."

"Fine, I'll leave, but this isn't the last time that you will see me. I can promise you that right now, Julie."

"Whatever you say, jerk."

After he left I went on with my business. I couldn't believe this dude. He was the one that was stalking me ever since I got into that fight with his brother. He was the one that was stopping me from starting a new life. I wanted to show the people that I run into from now on that I'm nice and I am nothing like my evil mother. I did want to try and get some decent sleep since I was running low on energy. I had no idea what time it was. My phone died and I had no way of charging it. That was the one problem with the woods. I had no electricity or heat. I had to get my light from the only other source I knew. That was the sun. By now the sun had gone down and so I was taking that as my signal that it was time to go to bed now. I found a nice branch up in a tree that I could sleep on. It was definitely going to be a challenge, but this wouldn't be the first time that I did this.

One day when I was ten years old my dad and I went on a father-daughter camping trip with a couple of friends. I was at the age where I refused to sleep on anything dirty. That included the ground I was going to have to sleep on. My dad came up with this brilliant idea that he would find a tree and I could sleep in that. Lucky enough he found like a little tree that had a platform attached to it. I slept in a tree that night. I didn't think this would be too different. The only thing that was different was that this tree didn't have a platform. I climbed up the tree and set my sleeping bag on the branch. I tied myself on the branch so I knew I wouldn't fall out. The difficult part about it was that the tree branch wasn't that wide, maybe twenty inches if I had to guess. I may not have been that good at math, but I did know one thing and that was twenty inches wasn't big at all. When I did get settled onto the branch and relaxed it was one of the most peaceful nights that I have had in a while. No owls, no night creatures, no nothing. It was just a nice cool fall night. I counted the stars to help me fall asleep. It was extravagant.

I will always remember that father daughter trip. It was one of the only moments that I felt like I had a father and that he loved me.

The next morning I got up and smelt pancakes. When I got down near the fire there was a plate full of pancakes. There was a note attached to the plate. The note said:

I am so sorry for last night. You were right. I was acting like a jerk just like my older brother. To apologize for my rudeness and my idiotic actions, I made pancakes this morning and brought some to you since I didn't know if you had anything yet to make for breakfast. I hope that you can and will accept these, as well as maybe we can become friends.

Sincerely,

Alexander

I don't know who this boy thought he was by making me pancakes just assuming that everything would be good between us. Well he thought wrong. Everything between us was definitely not good. Pancakes weren't going to make up for the way that he treated me last night. I wasn't going to be some pushover that would be nice to anyone that thought they could make it up to me by doing something extra to make up for their meanness. That was no way to treat a lady. I would show him how I work.

That next couple of hours I was busy planning my revenge. I knew exactly what was going to drive him up the wall. I had to somehow go find his campsite. It took me awhile be cause I kept running into dead ends. The woods had a lot of uphills, curvy turns and crazy paths. I finally found where he was set up and boy, was it beautiful! He has a tent, another clean pond, a fire, tons of food, and lastly a tree house that he built so he can get away if it is raining or just really cold. I couldn't ruin this. He must of worked forever to get it to look like this.

The only thing that I did want was some firewood. He had so much that I didn't think he would even notice if I took just a couple pieces of it. I looked around to make sure Alexander wasn't around at all. When I knew for a fact that he wasn't around I quickly went to go grab some firewood. I only took enough to last me for the afternoon. Then this evening around dinner I would go out myself to find some more. As soon as I headed back to my camp site I regretted it right away.

Chapter 5

When I got to my camp site all of it was ruined. The fire was gone, the berries were nowhere to be found, my bed was ruined, lastly all of my water was spilled all over the place. I couldn't believe it. I knew that there was only one person behind all of this. It had to be Alexander. Right beside my fire pit was another note. This note said:

I saw you heading to my camp site and I thought that you were going to ruin it and so I decided to do the same thing to you before you had the chance to do it to me. Here is to a fantastic start to what could be a wonderful friendship. If you want your water, bed, fruit, and fire to be all put back and fixed you have to find everything. I hid them all over the woods. Good luck.

Sincerely,

Alexander

This was just absolutely great. He was a total jerk. He was exactly like his brother and I knew that he wasn't ever going to change the way that he acted. There was no way on earth that I was going to forgive him. I tried my best to set up my campsite and now I have nothing. It seemed like anything I tried to do wasn't good enough and never will be.

This reminded me of when I was back with my mother. Whenever I would do anything for her it didn't matter if I did it perfectly or not she would always yell at me. I would always have to do the same thing two or three times before it was to her satisfaction. I didn't know how in the world I was going to be able to retrieve any of my stuff. The woods were ginormous. It would take me hours to search the whole premises of these woods. It took me two hours to just find the right space for me to begin with.

I wasn't going to fall for his trick. I knew exactly what he wanted me to do. He wanted me to run out of these woods so he had it all to himself. Well, it wasn't going to work. I wasn't going anywhere. I would just start all over. I came way too damn far to just give up. I couldn't believe any of this. If I wanted to start a new life then I couldn't even have him in my life, because all he wanted to do was get in the way and stop me. I decided to take the day to try and find a better spot in the woods of where there was no way that he would be able to find me. I gathered everything that was left of my stuff and headed deeper into the woods.

As soon as I started walking everything seemed to go back to being all nasty and gross. I didn't understand why that was. I thought that all the bad things that were happening to me were done with. I guessed wrong apparently. Where I walked all of the flowers were dead and the smell in the surrounding area was atrocious. Then I ran into dead animals like snakes, deer, baby bears, rats and every other forest animals you could imagine. I thought to myself why would anyone want to kill animals like this and then just leave them in the woods like this. Then again I only knew two people that were in these woods and that was me and the evil, despicable, nasty, jerk face Alexander. The woods didn't get any prettier as I went. I was half determined to just go back to my original camp site and hope that Alexander would just leave me alone. I decided to head back.

When I got to the campsite all of my hope was lost. Alexander was already there and so I went to spy on him. He took my campsite so he deserved to be spied on. I found some camouflage clothing in my bag.

I climbed up in a tree high enough so Alexander wouldn't be able to see me. It looked like he was having an amazing time ruining my campsite and making it his little own. It was like he knew I was watching him. He tried to make everything that I had better. For example, the fire that I made was only a little fire enough to keep me warm and heat little things up to eat but his was much bigger. He had baskets of fruits and nuts when I could barely even find a handful of them. Then he had an actual tent to sleep in when I only had a sleeping bag. I couldn't understand where he was getting all of these things from searching the woods. He had some kind of superpower or something that I didn't have.

I was trying to be super quiet so he didn't know I was watching him. Well, that plan didn't work out the way that I wanted it to. My foot slipped off a branch and like lightning I stumbled down right behind him making a huge boom sound. He quickly looked around to try and find me. I was quick enough to pull myself to the other side of the tree so he wasn't able to see me. I did see that it was making him mad though because he knew that someone or something was watching him. It was amazing seeing him frustrated. He was running around like a crazy maniac looking everywhere. High and low and to each side.

As soon as I saw that Alexander was settled and back into his tent I quietly climbed out from behind the tree and went around his campsite to explore a little more. There had to be some secret of how he was getting all of this stuff. I mean yes, he has been in these woods longer then I have been, but I thought that I had better surviving skills then he did. The reasoning for my thinking is because when I first met him it looked like he hasn't had a bath or anything in a long while. That is the one thing that I couldn't understand since there was a pond just a little way into the woods. It was closer to his first campsite before than it was now. I know it isn't the cleanest water there could possibly be, but it did help me a lot when I went to get cleaned up. I didn't care what I had to do but I had to get to the end of all the madness and craziness one way or another.

By the time I got to Alexander's last campsite it was bare. Nothing that was there before was there anymore. I couldn't understand how he could have moved everything in such a short amount of time. He had to have received some kind of help that I didn't know about. There was no logical way that he could have moved and found everything all by himself. The best way to figure out if he was the only one or if there was someone else around was to watch him overnight to see if I could find anything suspicious. I first set up a mini camera that I had and then I went into the tree that I watched Alexander from during the day to set up my sleeping bag.

Watching Alexander at night was an entertaining sight for the first couple of hours. He was in his tent doing something bizarre. I didn't know what he was doing though.

It looked like he was talking to someone, but I knew that there wasn't anyone else in the tent with him. He was also flapping his arms in the air like a crazy person. Similar to earlier this morning when it was driving him insane not knowing who or what was watching him. I kinda overlooked it though and laid back down in the tree. At about three in the morning something weird did happen. It was really creepy because there was a lot of noise and it woke me up. More noise than when he was talking to someone else in the tent, which I still believe he was just talking to himself because I knew for a fact that there was no one else in the tent with him.

All of a sudden Alexander quickly ran out of his tent and started up the fire again. It was like he thought that someone was going to do something bad to him. He had to find some firewood. The strange thing was that there was firewood that was getting put in the fire, but he wasn't the one picking it up and putting it in. It was being lifted in mid air. I couldn't believe my eyes. I didn't know what was making that happen. For a minute I thought that he had some kind of magic powers. Then again that was impossible. There was no such thing as magic. The only other thing that I could think of is it was some kind of special effect. The kind you see in the plays and on television. Another thing that I didn't know was how he would be able to do any kind of special effects because in the woods there is no electricity or reasons for special effects.

I just wanted to believe that all of this was just a dream and that if I would go back to sleep and then wake up then none of this be true. It was just so crazy that if I told anyone then they wouldn't believe me for the slightest of a minute. None of this made any sense to me even. I didn't want to believe that I was going crazy. I wasn't like my mom and didn't want to be like her. She was the top level of crazy. I decided to go back to sleep and hope for the best.

Chapter 6

When I woke up I couldn't believe my eyes. Everything was gone again! There was no sight of Alexander anywhere. It was like he wasn't even there the day before. I went to try and see if he moved back to his original campsite. When I got there it was even more empty than the other campsite. It was so strange. All of this was making me think that I was truly turning crazy. I knew I wasn't, but it was all of the events that were occurring which was making my mind think that I was. I decided to eat a little because maybe not eating was having an effect on what my mind was seeing. There had to be some reason that Alexander was acting like that and then all of a sudden disappearing like he did.

While I was eating I heard a big, loud and nasty sound. It sounded like a gunshot to me. I quickly gathered up my stuff and ran. I didn't want to take the chance of getting shot or killed. Especially with all the weird mysterious things that have been happening. I ran all the way out of the woods. As soon as I was far enough out of the woods I stopped to take a break. I knew I had to find somewhere else to stay. The woods were not right. I didn't know if Alexander had anything to do with the things, but all I knew is if I stayed there any longer there was a possible chance that I wouldn't make it out of the woods alive.

I started walking to try and find another place that I could stay. After about an hour I found a small town. The town was so small that there were only two cars that I could see. I was wondering why the town was as small as it was. Maybe it had something to do with the supernatural events that happened in and around the woods. I went into a small store. There was no one in the store. There was a sign on the window that said: If no one is here please just take what you want. Don't worry about paying.

That made no sense at all. Why would anyone just give away things if no one was there. I wanted to be honest and pay, but I had no money and I haven't had that much to eat since the morning before everything happened. I only took what I truly needed.

The store looked like it was about to go out of business. Everything was gray, silent, no emotion at all, everything was dusty and stiff, and last but not least there were rats and mice running all over the place. I took a look around and they barely had anything left. They needed to get more inventory.

When I went into the back room there was absolutely nothing. It was definitely dirty though and not the most sanitary place there was. I thought to myself though that if no one was in the store then maybe I could stay there at least for tonight. I went to go find a broom and some other cleaning supplies to see if I could clean the store up just a little bit. I didn't want to take the chance of getting sick or get any diseases, especially since there were rats and mice running all over the damn place. Who knows what kinds of things those tiny, nasty, annoying and mean creatures carried. I set up a couple mouse traps that I found in the one closet.

I did find some food that wasn't expired so I made that for my dinner. They didn't have a oven or anything so I just had fruit, granola bars and juice. Everything was pretty good to my surprise. After I was done eating I made sure I locked all the doors and turned off all the lights before I went to bed to ensure that no one would be able to get in. The reason for this was to make sure that no one knew that I was even staying there. I was hoping that this plan was going to work. I do have to admit that it was a very risky plan, but I knew if I was just very secretive about it all then there was no chance that I would get caught. I set my sleeping bag up and went right to sleep. I slept so peacefully. It was amazing. I don't know what time I got up though since there were no clocks around at all. The only thing I knew was it was rainy and windy. It looked like it would be a good day to stay in the store and maybe clean it up a little. I never knew if anyone could come back here after I leave. It was going to be a long day I could already tell.

After about two hours of it storming all of the power went out. It went completely dark. I wasn't ready for that. This place didn't have any extra lamps or anything in case of emergencies like this. It was disappointing. I didn't know what to do since this town was very small and it was storming hard.

I finally did find a little flashlight that I could use. At first it didn't work and I got frustrated. I threw the flashlight down on the ground and it flickered on. I was in luck. At least I had some light to use so I could do things and not just sit around the store worrying about what was going to happen next. I decided to continue reading my book that I brought from home. I read for a good couple of hours when all of a sudden I heard the door come knocking down. I got scared for my life. I threw the closest thing that was near me and that was a box of various fruits. It wasn't the best choice, but I didn't know what else to do.

There was no way that people knew that I was staying in this gross and nasty place. Who could it have been though? That is one question that ran through my head. As soon as the person was down because of the box of fruit hitting them I got up and ran as far as I could. This town for sure had paranormal activities going on. It seemed like everything and everywhere I went it got stranger and stranger. I just needed to find one place and stay there. It was raining so hard that I didn't want to do any walking, but I knew that I had to. It was for my safety and best interest.

My bag got soaked while all of my belongings got to stay dry. In the middle of my walk I heard a faint whisper, "I am following you and always will." It scared me really bad. It was such a faint voice though. It couldn't of even been a person that said it because it sounded like it was right above or in front of me and the voice was too soft. It drove me crazy. I knew it was my mind trying to trick me into thinking that I wasn't alone even though I knew I was. The voice kept talking to me. The thing that it said that drove me absolutely crazy was, "You are paranoid and don't hear anything. You are going to end up just like your demented mother."

At that point I was beyond angry. I was pissed off. I

yelled at the top of my lungs, "I AM NOT LIKE MY MOTHER AND NEVER WILL BE!" As soon as I said that I just broke down crying. I couldn't believe everything that I was going through.

The only thing that I could think that was causing all of these things is that Alexander was behind every single thing. I don't know why or how he would be, but that was the only thing that I could think of. The only reason my mind was thinking this was because whenever Alexander was around everything good was happening. Then the moment that I leave him and he disappears my life turns to crap again. This was ridiculous, that was one thing for sure. I just needed to get away from all human race. I knew that wasn't possible, but that seemed like that was what would work for me.

I wanted to give up. I didn't know what to do next.

Chapter 7

I kept picking up the pace. Not knowing where I was going or where I wanted to end up. The voice still didn't leave me alone, but I just decided to leave it alone and ignore it. I may or may not have known where it came from. I did stop a couple times just to rest and because I was still soaked from the rain and just wanted to sit in loneliness. This is where I belonged. When the dark came I decided to just find somewhere to lay. I didn't care where or if it was going to stay dry for me the whole night, I just wanted sleep. When I laid down I fell right to sleep.

In the middle of the night I felt warm all of a sudden even though it was freezing. I didn't know what it was, but I honestly couldn't care less so I didn't even wake up to see what was happening. I stayed like that for the rest of the night.

The next morning I yelled at the top of my lungs because here to find out in some mysterious way Alexander showed up and found me. Apparently, he saw me and thought it was going to be okay with me if he came and slept with me through the night. It took me a few moments to wake up and realize that it was him. As soon as I came to my senses I went off.

"What the hell are you doing?"

"I thought you looked cold and could use some company!"

"Well, you are so totally wrong. I was doing just fine without you. I thought I lost you."

"You thought wrong then, Julie. I will never leave you."

"Why is that?"

"Because I can help you. You are just so damn stubborn that you won't let me help you."

"Have you ever thought that maybe I don't need any help. Especially from a guy like you. You are just getting in my way. My life would be so much better if you weren't in it."

"Well, that was kinda rude, young lady."

"I don't care. I don't need or want your help now, just please leave me alone and stay out of my life"

"Never!"

I ran after he said that to try and get away from him. I knew that was never going to happen, but it was worth a try. I knew he was the reason that everything was happening. I didn't want to ask him or try to figure him out. It was going to be more work on my part. I kept going. One thing that was different though is after Alexander left the voice went away. It went back to peace and quiet. The way I like it.

Everything seemed to be normal for the next hour or so. Then something out of the ordinary happened. There came a small garden. There was a sign that said *"Community Garden."* It was about a mile away from a different little town. It was gorgeous. It was nicely maintained as well. All the flowers were bloomed, the mulch was kept nicely, and the beautiful rocks that were around the border of the garden where it was nicely in order. There was a nice little spot between the flowers that I could sit down and enjoy myself. I did exactly that. I didn't care if I wasn't supposed to or not, I was getting restless. I didn't want to walk anymore. Especially since I didn't have anywhere specific I was heading. I just wanted to find somewhere to settle down. I knew that wasn't going to work.

I had no idea where I was even at. I knew I wasn't in New York City anymore. The reason I knew that is because New York City is always busy and noisy. I had to be in some state that wasn't as loud or busy. All I was seeing was a couple of buildings that looked new, newly paved roads, and then there was this garden that had flowers like Calla's Chrysanthemums, Leptospermums and Lilies. It was a sight to see. I just wanted to know where I was.

I was so lonely. Maybe Alexander's company wouldn't be as bad as I thought. It's just he was so annoying and mean. If he was anything like his brother though I didn't want him around me. I already have a black eye and if bullying ran in his family who knows what other kind of injuries I would run into. I thought I would leave Alexander a note apologizing for how I acted.

Dear Alexander,

I'm so sorry of how I acted towards you. I honestly didn't intend to be so mean. I just am lost and confused as well as trying to find my dad. Your brother just gave me a good idea of how your family is. I shouldn't have assumed that you were like your brother. I hope you find this note. I'm so sorry.

Sincerely,

Julie

I nicely folded the letter and put it between some of the flowers. I had no idea if Alexander would find it though. I was really hoping that he would come walking the same path I did and find the note. I don't know why he wouldn't. He did follow me all the way from his house until now. He did have good stalking skills though. He had a way of knowing every single step I took and kept his distance so he knew I wouldn't be able to see him following me. I couldn't keep thinking about that at this moment. My mind had other things on it. I think I was starting to hallucinate. I was starting to see double of everything.

I was getting to be hungry and really thirsty. I had no food or water left. I had nothing else with me. I wish I would've packed more food or been more prepared. I guess I was in too much of a hurry to get away from my mother.

I wondered what she was doing that moment. She had to know that I wasn't there anymore. It had been five days since I left. Maybe with me being gone she actually got off her ass to get some things done so she could better herself. She was so unhealthy because she was having me do everything for her. I was so glad I was gone. Now maybe I could actually get better myself, since according to my mother I needed help. I refused to get help though. I had in my mind that I could help myself by getting away from everything that was causing me to stress. That was the one thing I didn't have that much of when I was out here in nature. The only things that were causing me to stress were Alexander and all the strange phenomenal things that were happening. I was hoping that the Alexander part would stop if he could find the note and then come to find me. I just wish all of this craziness would stop. I couldn't take it anymore.

It was starting to get colder and darker. I felt like I was going to die of starvation and dehydration. I was about to lay down when all of a sudden a water bottle came rolling and hitting my leg. I didn't even question it. I was so thirsty that I needed something to drink. I drank all of the water in less than thirty seconds. When I looked back I saw him. I didn't know what to think except to go up and hug him. I was so glad to see him. I finally wasn't alone anymore. I could finally stop stressing so much.

"I'm so glad to see you, Alexander."

"You are? That was a quick attitude change."

"Yes, I am so happy to see you. Did you get my note? I left it by the tree in the garden"

"Yes, I got your note."

"Okay, well I am glad that you got the note. Now that you read the note hopefully I have something to ask you."

"What is it, Julie?"

"Will you walk with me for the rest of my journey? I made a mistake of pushing you away. I now realize that you can be very helpful along the way. I am so stubborn sometimes that I don't see that I need help when I actually do."

"Of course I will stay with you the rest of the way, Julie. You look extremely tired though. I think you may need to stop for the day to get some rest. I don't want to see anything bad happen to you just because you get sick or are tired."

"Yeah. Maybe you are right. I think I'll just go to sleep for the night."

"Do you want me to sleep with you so you don't have to be so lonely?"

"Sure, but I don't think we will be lonely. I forgot to mention that there is some kind of voice that has been following me. It comes and goes. I never know when it will come again."

"Whatever you say, Julie. Just close your eyes and get some sleep."

After he told me that I quietly got my sleeping bag ready. I got in and made sure that there was enough room for Alexander. As soon as I was falling asleep Alexander crawled in with me. It felt weird at first, but as soon as he put his arm around me I felt comfortable and safe.

Chapter 8

I slept really good again. Maybe that was because I knew Alexander was with me for most of the evening. The only thing that was weird was when I got up was Alexander wasn't beside me. He did leave me a note though. The note said:

Hey Julie.

I got up early so I could maybe go find us some food. If you need something before I get back just say it out loud and I will get your message. Don't question how I will get this information or anything. I will explain a lot of your questions when I get back. All you need to know for right now is you will always be safe even if I'm not with you. I'll see you in a little bit. Just relax and read your book.

Love,

Alexander

I had no idea what to take from all of that. Maybe he would explain what all the weird events were and why they were happening. I was hoping because I wanted to go to bed one night knowing that all of this wasn't in my head and I wasn't going crazy like my mother. Anyways, I listened to what Alexander told me in the letter and relaxed while reading my book. The one thing that I thought was weird is how he knew that I had a book with me. I never showed or told him that I had it. It was always in my bag because it was way gigantic and heavy to carry it everywhere. Also the bag protects it from harsh conditions.

Only about a half hour had passed before Alexander got back to where I was. I didn't know he got back because I was intensely reading. He came behind me and put his hands over my eyes. When he did that I jumped up and gave him a huge hug. I was so glad he was back. When I looked behind him he had a lot - food, water, firewood, and everything we needed to survive. I had no idea how in the world he got it all. I didn't even bother questioning him about it though. Before I said a word he took me by the hand and sat me down. He had a lot to tell me.

"Julie. I need to be completely and openly honest with you. I am not who you think I am. I come from a very rich and wealthy family."

"Then why on earth are you out here in the middle of nowhere? You could be at home living up the life and not having to worry about a single thing. When you are out here you don't have a single thing."

"The reason for that is because I hate how my family is treating me. They treat me like a little kid. They don't let me do anything. I have no freedom a lot of the time. I am home-schooled. I usually have to get up, do my school work, then I have a farm that I have to take care of. I also have five little siblings. They all have either piano, dance, horseback riding or another activity that they do and I have to take and pick them all up from everything. My parents do help me with some things, but most of these things I have to do. It truly sucks. I bet you don't know what it is like."

"Well, you are wrong, Alexander. I do know what is is like. See, my father left me when I was fourteen years old. I am seventeen right now. Ever since he left my life has been a living hell. My mother became depressed and basically locked herself in her room. She made me do everything. I had to enroll in online schooling so there wasn't a chance that I would leave the house. I have tried everything in my power to leave that damn house, but there was no chance for me. I finally did manage to escape but that's because I finally realized that I wasn't going to be able to get out of that situation if I didn't take any action. I have always talked the talk, but I never put actions to my words. Since I finally did escape I decided to go on this wild adventure. Then it has been this one wild long journey. Now do you think I don't know what you are going through?"

"Oh my gosh, Julie. I had no idea. I'm sorry. I thought you were a girl trying to ruin her own life by running away from home."

"Well, I'm not. I could say the same thing about you too, Alexander. Now next time will you please find out your facts before you go around assuming things."

"Okay. I am so sorry again, Julie. I promise next time I will actually gather the facts from you before I go and assume things. I should know better. My brother always did the same thing and it has landed him in deep trouble."

"Wait, so does your older brother live with you? You said that you have five younger siblings and your brother is definitely not younger than you."

"No. My brother Jason does not live with me. He comes to visit us a lot though. He moved out when he was around seventeen. He got involved with drugs, alcohol, sex, and gangs. When he moved out he moved in with his "girlfriend" of that day. I will give him credit though. This girlfriend lasted a lot longer than most of his girlfriends. They broke up after they were together for a year. The reason for that was he got drunk one night and beat the hell out of her. After she got out of the hospital she filed a restraining order against him. That was the last time he has heard or seen that girl. Which if you ask me that was the best thing for the both of them."

"Oh wow, okay. I agree with you that might of been the best thing for the both of them from what I hear."

"Thanks for agreeing with me, Julie. That means a lot to me. This is the first time that someone has actually taken the time and listened to me about that situation. Another thing is I ran away from home because I didn't want to end up like my brother. My brother got it from our parents. They would usually go out once a month and stay out all night drinking. Then when they would come home the next morning they would be totally hungover. I believe that is where my brother got it from. My parents would always leave beer or something around and my brother would sneak it when they weren't around. I tried to stop him, but he wouldn't listen since he was the oldest. I never really thought about drinking, but knew that I had to get away from it while I still have control over what I do."

"That was a good choice, Alexander. You are welcome

for listening. I know what it is like not to be listened to. Now that we know each other a little better do you want to stay here or do you want to continue walking and see if we can get anywhere else."

"Well, I hate to say this but I have to go. I can't stay. I can't tell you why I can't stay. All you need to know is that you will be okay. I have faith in you."

"What? You can't stay?"

"I'm sorry, Julie."

I gave him a big hug and let a couple tears out. I didn't want him to go. I didn't want to be lonely again. I insisted on going with him though. I wouldn't let go of his arm. We tugged each other back and forth. I wouldn't admit it to him but I was kinda starting to like him. He finally got me off of him by pushing me to the ground. That hurt. Now I was starting to wonder if he was like his brother. Especially since he was starting to get physical.

As soon as I closed my eyes and opened them again he was gone. I still didn't know how he was gone so fast. He left another note behind though. This time the note didn't just include words. There was also a picture with it. I didn't know what the picture was exactly though. This is what the note said:

I'm so sorry, Julie. I just couldn't stay at all. I had some other business that I had to take care of. I promise this won't be the last time we see each other. I don't know when I will be back. It could be days, weeks, months or years. I have no idea. It all depends on what I have to do. I love you and always will. I will always know if you are okay or not. You will know what I mean when the time is right. I hope you will understand. Talk to you soon.

Love,

Alexander

P.S the drawing is supposed to be a silly picture of friends. I hope that can give you some insight of how I want to be with you."

Alexander's note made no sense at all. What was it supposed to mean? Maybe he meant he wanted to be closer friends. Even if that was the case that was insane. I didn't like Alexander in that way. I already promised myself I wasn't going to get into a relationship until I was stable enough and stable was something that I wasn't. I didn't want to believe that part of the note. The only thing that I believed was this wasn't going to be the last time that I saw Alexander. I knew that he was a man of his word. He could be a jerk at times but I have never known him to be a liar. I just don't think I could go without seeing him for more than a couple days. I was really hoping that he would only be gone for a couple of days. I had no way of telling though. I was hoping he was staying safe and making the right choices. I didn't want anything bad happening to him. Last but not least I didn't want him to end up like his brother. That was my number one concern. All I could do was hope for the best.

Chapter 9

As days went on I started to miss Alexander a lot. I couldn't stand the thought of not being able to see him for a long while. The voice that was a part of my imagination kept coming and going. That is what really triggered me to miss everything about Alexander. His voice, his sense of humor, his caring attitude, sympathy, and his mean but kind self. Everything was burning in the back of my mind. Half of me kept thinking that he was gathering food for us and then he would be back any minute and we would spend the day arguing back and forth, but at the end of the day we would cuddle up in my sleeping bag and just sleep peacefully throughout the night. That was my thought of a perfect day and night in my mind. Now that he was gone I didn't have any of that. I was all alone.

One day I decided to try and make friends with the voice. That seemed like the only logical thing to do so I wouldn't be lonely. Most of the time when I tried to talk it was only me talking. The voice didn't want to talk that much. It listened though. I knew it was listening because I could feel the presence of it somehow. I considered the voice a friend. It was the only one that would listen to all my complaining. The voice one day actually had a conversation with me.

"Julie, please don't be scared. I know what you are going through. I know I haven't spoke before but I decided to finally speak today. You have no reason to be scared. "

At first when the voice said something I jumped. I was really shocked. I didn't think the voice would ever talk back to me when I tried having a conversation with it. I then decided to try and talk to the voice.

"Hi. I don't know your name. What is your name?"

It didn't say anything at first. After about ten minutes it spoke to me again. "I don't have a name. I am part of your imagination. When you think of someone being here with you I will show up. I am here to help you not think of Alexander while he is gone. I am not wanting to hurt you. I am wanting to help you through your journey. Is that okay with you?"

"Yes, that is okay with me, I guess. Am I the only one that can hear you and understand you?"

"That is all up to you, Julie. If you want to tell people about me then that is totally okay with me."

"Okay, well thank you. I am not going to be telling people about you because I only have one thing to tell you. I really don't need anyone's help. I can take care of my own self. I have been for the past three years. No matter what life throws my way I can handle it myself. While it was nice talking to you and getting to know you I will no longer need you. You can leave me alone and never bother me again."

"Whatever you say, Julie. I will no longer talk to you if that is what you want."

"Yes, that is what I want. I want you out of my life. This is crazy and I will not end up like my lunatic mother."

The voice didn't say anything after that. I was really hoping that whoever he or she was they would just leave me alone and not bother me again, even though it was nice to have someone to talk to and not judge me for my past. I was hoping that all of it was in my head. I didn't or couldn't analyze why any of this was happening or if any of it really made any sense at all. I started thinking and maybe I did need some professional help. I got my computer out to start searching for people that I could maybe start seeing. I didn't find much. The only person I found was Doctor Ramirez. She was located in a town called Homerville. I had no clue where it was or where I was. Luckily I could use my laptop to charge my phone just enough so I could figure out where in the world I was and where this town was. When my phone got charged it looked like I barely had any service, but just enough to find out that I had to travel five miles to the next closest town.

It was already getting dark so I decided to get a good night's sleep and then I would get to the town in the morning. It was the best choice in my opinion. I carefully got settled into bed and just watched all the stars come out. I listened to the wind that was gently blowing. It was such a peaceful night. I enjoyed it while I could since I didn't know when the next time there would be another peaceful night like this.

During the night it was not like all of the other nights. It started to rain a little. It didn't pour down rain but it sprinkled. It wasn't cold. That was the strange part. Since it was a warm night out I did take my shirt off but I wrapped my shirt around me so I wasn't shirtless. The rain felt incredible on my skin. I haven't felt this kind of sensation in a while. The last time I felt this good was the last night that Alexander was with me. I had another dream about him. This time the dream was us on our wedding day.

It was a warm June afternoon. Our wedding took place on a beach in Florida. The theme was America and so everything was red, white, and blue. It was about twenty minutes until I had to walk down the aisle. Alexander did something out of the ordinary and came up behind me with his eyes closed to kiss me. As soon as that part happened I woke up from the dream. That was another dream that I didn't want to wake up from, but when I did it was already morning.

That morning I started my journey to try and find this damn town. There wasn't much to walk on. The only direction I could go was straight. It was all dust and dryness behind me. I didn't understand how one place could get so dry and hot. It was ridiculous. I just wanted to get away from this place and into an air conditioned place. To make the walk a little quicker I kept thinking of how much happier I was now then I ever was at my old home.

I did have to admit that I missed having a familiar place to sleep at night. I missed the comfort of being able to get up knowing that I would have food to eat. I would also have a place where I could take a shower and get cleaned instead of being dirty. When I was at the house I did have the opportunity to have WiFi, electricity, heat, and air conditioning whenever I needed. Those are the only main things that I missed. I for sure didn't miss my mother demanding things from me all the time. I always had to do all the chores around the house. I had to cook every single meal every single day. At first it was fun since I liked to cook. My dad had taught me most everything I needed to know for cooking. If it wasn't for him I don't think I would be where I am now. I also didn't miss the getting up extra early to get school done just so I could get the house extra clean for some special event or occasion. Those were the days that I hated the most. By the time I got done daydreaming I was at the next town.

It was a lot bigger than the last one. It actually had people in it. Maybe my hopes of finding somewhere to stay was bigger than I thought it would be. When I got into the town I heard some people talking. The language was different though. It definitely wasn't English. I heard someone say "Esta ciudad es tan hermoso y sorprendente." I knew that was Spanish, and the only way I knew that was because I took a Spanish course online. It meant "This town is so beautiful and amazing". I was pretty good at Spanish so trying to communicate with people wasn't going to be a problem for me. I just had to find someone that looked like they could help me. This was going to be a challenge.

Chapter 10

I finally found a girl that looked like my age. This girl was tall, skinny, with gorgeous brown hair, and absolutely beautiful blue eyes. I went up to her to see if I could get a conversation going. I first decided to try English to see if this person knew any.

"Hi. Can you help me?"

No one answered. To me that meant that this person didn't know any English which meant that I would have to speak Spanish.

"Hola. Mi nombre es Julie." *Hi. My name is Julie.*

"Hola, Julie. Mi nombre es Monica." *Hi, Julie. My name is Monica.*

"Es un placer conocerte, Monica. Soy de la Ciudad de New York. Me preguntaba si podrica mostrar el camino a la oficina de los médicos más cercanos." *It's nice to meet you, Monica. I am from New York City. I was wondering if you could show me to the closest doctor's office.*

"Si. Esta justo al lado de la calle." *Yes. It is right across the street.*

"Muchas gracias, Mónica. Mejor me voy." *Thank you so much, Monica. I better get going.*

"De acuerdo, Julie." *Okay, Julie.*

As soon as I got directions on where to go I went to the doctor's office to see if they could either help me or guide me to who I needed to go see. When I walked into the doctor's office the waiting room was beautiful. It had an extravagant chandelier, pretty blue walls, nice wooden floors, a huge desk and nice chairs. I went up to the receptionist and tried again with the English. To my relief this person did speak English.

"Hi. May I speak to someone who can help me."

"Hi. How may I help you?"

"I am looking for a therapist or at least someone who can guide me where to go. I am not from here and need someone."

"Well, you came to the right place. We have a therapist who is at the office at all times. May I have your name and I will have someone come out to get you."

"Yes. My name is Julie."

"Thank you, Julie. Now if you go and wait someone will be out with you shortly. If you could fill out this paperwork while you are waiting, and give it to the doctor, it will save time."

"Thank you so much."

I sat down to fill out the paperwork, which was the usual stuff about medical history, symptoms, allergies and such. It didn't take me long to finish. While I was waiting I picked up some of the magazines that they had out. I grabbed the first one that was on top of the pile. The title of it was *"New Jersey First Hand."* That finally explained where I was and why there were a lot of people who spoke Spanish, since I knew that some parts of the state almost twenty percent of the population spoke Spanish. It was interesting to find out some facts about New Jersey. Of course when I got into reading the doctor came out to get me. When I went into her office I sat down in this big comfy chair. She was so nice but she was soft spoken though. I could barely hear what she was saying.

"Hi. My name is Doctor Ramirez. How may I help you?"

"Hi. My name is Julie. I looked you up on the internet because I decided that I needed to talk to a therapist."

"Well, you came to the right place. Now what is your situation?"

"I will start from the beginning. About three years ago my dad left me and my mom. After he left, my mom went into a deep depression. Which when that happened my mom basically locked herself in her room and made me her slave. I had to do everything for her and she wouldn't leave her room. I became depressed when she started that because I had no freedom. Then about a week and a half ago I had enough and decided to run away. I first tried to find my dad, but when I traveled three towns over I gave up thinking that there was no way of finding him. I then decided to give up.

"As I kept making my way to somewhere I could stay there was this boy who magically appeared in the woods where I decided to stay. Then when I told him to leave there was a voice that I started to hear. I didn't really think anything about it. After a couple days this boy ran me out of the woods.

I stayed in this abandoned store that I found in a little town. The next day when I about got killed by someone I ran and just started walking. That is when a lot of things happened that I think is just in my head. I finally decided to come find someone to help me. That is why I am here."

"Oh wow, Julie. That is a lot to take in. I am glad you came and found me. How old are you?"

"I am seventeen. I will be eighteen in two months."

"Okay Julie. Since you are almost eighteen years old I can help you without a parent being with you, as they are in a different state, and part of your problems. You will have to go into a half-way house until you've reached the age of 18, and proved you are responding well to treatment. I think the best place for you for the time being is in a hospital. There they will give you tests and then you will be put on medication. You will be safe there. You won't have to worry about anything."

"That sounds like a good plan. I honestly believe that will help me. I am sick and tired of being this way."

"Okay, I will call them and they will come and pick you up so that you don't have to worry about getting there."

"Thank you, Doctor Ramirez."

When I was sitting in the waiting room I fell asleep for a few minutes. I had a really weird dream. The dream was about how I was in the middle of the North Pole freezing to death. I was literally in the middle of nowhere. There were no cities, no villages, no nothing. I was surrounded by snow.

During my dream there was a huge snow storm that started and I got stuck in a huge pile of snow. I couldn't move or anything. My limbs started to freeze and then I blacked out. After that I woke up screaming. Both the receptionist and therapist came running into the room to check on me.

"Julie! What in the world happened? You scared me!" said Dr. Ramirez.

"Yes, I am fine. I just fell asleep and had a really bad dream."

"Don't worry, Julie, we are going to help you get better."

"I know you guys are. Thank you."

After that the people from the hospital came through the door to get me. I got taken to the hospital in an ambulance. When I got settled into the back of the ambulance they took my blood pressure, took my temperature, checked my heart rate, and then gave me some water to drink. It only took about twenty minutes to get to the hospital. When I got there they took me into a room. I didn't like the room at all. It didn't have anything in it. No television, no windows, no outlets or anything. There was only a bed and a door. A doctor came in my room and took everything from me. Apparently, until they took tests and the results came back I wasn't allowed to have anything with me. I thought it was stupid, but if it was to help me then I was going to accept it. Since I didn't have anything with me I decided to go back to sleep. I regretted it though. I had the same dream again. This time I woke up before the huge snow storm even started. I counted that part as the worse thing that could ever happen to me. When the doctors heard me screaming they came rushing in.

When they asked me what was wrong and I told them that I had a bad dream they sent a therapist in to talk to me.

"Hi Julie. I am Ms. Lay. I am the therapist here at the hospital. I came in to talk to you and give you a few tests. What made you scream?"

"I had a dream that I was being abandoned."

"Have you ever had moments you were or felt like you were in real life?"

"Yes, when my dad left me."

"Okay. Here is what is going to happen. I am going to have you take some tests for me."

"Okay."

Ms. Lay then gave me three paper tests. They asked me questions that dealt with topics like; family, friends, school, coping skills, and myself. It took half an hour for each test. When I was done I had to wait for my test results. My results took longer than all three tests combined. I was given paper to draw on while I was waiting. After about three hours Ms. Lay came back in.

"Julie, I have some new for you."

"What is it?"

"You are going to have to spend the night in the hospital because of what the tests are starting to show. I can't tell you quite yet what the test results are, but staying in the hospital is the best thing for you right now."

"Well, if it is the best for me right now then I'm going to have to accept it. Thank you, Ms. Lay."

I spent the next few hours in the hospital.

Chapter 11

The hospital took very good care of me. Ms. Lay put me on a 24 hour watch since she didn't want me to do anything stupid. I was finally able to get some sleep unlike I have been ever since I left my mother's. I took a three hour nap until the doctors came in to make sure that I eat.

I ate all of the food that they gave me. I was starving. I didn't think I would ever see good food again. The doctors were surprised that I ate as much as I did. Then the doctors took me back into the same room that I went in when I first got to the hospital. In there I just relaxed and ate the rest of what I had. I was so glad that the testing was done and I could relax waiting to hear what the test results came back as. After about three hours the doctors came in to talk to me.

"Julie. We analyzed the test that you took."

"What did the results come back as?"

"We discovered that you have what we call PTSD - Post-traumatic Stress Disorder." The doctor said with a disappointing look on her face.

"What does that mean?"

"That means that after seeing things that happened with your dad and then the past few years living with your mom it triggered something in your mind and it made you go into an extensive depression as well as anxiety, which is all exacerbated by various triggers. It is called Post-traumatic

Stress Disorder. Since you have struggled with events from your past and have had bad dreams about the events it has triggered you. Also you have tried to avoid everything from running away from home. That isn't going to fix anything, but you have done the right thing by coming to seek help."

"Is this something that can be cured or will I just have to deal with it for the rest of my life?"

"No, hopefully you will not have to deal with this for the rest of your life. It can be cured with a combination of medicine and counseling. It will also take you being willing to get better."

"Does that mean that I will have to be in this hospital for a couple months?"

"No. We will be sending you to a group home where they will help you. They will make sure you stay on track with medications, help you get a job, help you graduate, and lastly they will make sure you will be able to be stable when you are finally allowed to be out on your own. That way when you are done with treatments you will hopefully be able to get your own house or apartment."

"Okay. That sounds really good. What will happen if I have another episode like I did at the therapist's office before I came here?"

"Yes. If you have another episode like you did then you will most likely end up back here. Along with Zoloft I will be prescribing Clonazepam to help ease your anxiety and help you sleep a lot better. It also should help you though not to have another episode like that. You will take Zoloft and Clonazepam for three weeks and then you will come back to see another therapist in town to check in on how you are doing. Your group home will help you recover. You will be transported to the house today after lunch."

After the doctor left I took my first dose of medicine. I went to take a nap before I had to leave. I was surprised that I didn't have another nightmare. It felt amazing. I could actually control my dreams. I didn't think that it would ever happen again. I used to be able to when I was younger. Then for some reason after my dad left I wasn't able to anymore. I was angry when that happened. I couldn't wait to see how this medicine worked. When I got up I was so relaxed. When I was finally picked up to be taken to the house it felt like I was a new me. I never felt as comfortable as I did when I woke up.

When I got to the house there was a lady that greeted me at the front door. The house was huge! It was a brick house with a pretty blue paint. It was like a house you would see in a "perfect neighborhood." In my sight this house would be my dream home. I couldn't wait to see what was in store for me when I walked through the doors.

"Hi, Julie. My name is Mary. I am the lady that owns this house and will be here every day to help you with your recovery. My motto is *Together We Can Get Things Done.*"

"Hi, Mary. I'm glad to be here and start my recovery. I promise you I will try my best while I am at this house so I can get better. I know that you only want what is best for me."

"Good. I am glad that you feel this way, Julie. Here let me take your bags and show you to your room."

We went upstairs to a pink room. There was another girl in there already. I thought to myself that this was going to be interesting because I have never shared a room in my life. I didn't know what to expect. Mary kept talking and I just put everything on the back burner because I didn't want to share a room.

"This is Hailey. She is another one of the teens in the house. We have four teens in total. Three girls and one boy. I don't know where they are right now. I hope Hailey will kindly help you settle into your room. You girls will be sharing the room together. We will be having a meeting here at five. Hailey will tell you the routine that everyone is required to do each day."

"Thank you, Mary."

As soon as Mary left it went silent in the room for a few moments. I put my clothes that I did have in the dresser that was provided. I finally broke the silence between Hailey and I.

"Hi, Hailey. I am Julie."

"What do you want?" Hailey said with a sassy attitude.

"What is up with you? All I said was hi. I'm just trying to be nice and get to know what I should expect while I am here."

"Well, I am sorry. I'm not in a good mood. I don't want to share my room with anyone new. I have already went through this once before. I have been in here for four years

75

and the girl that was here before you was only here for three months before she got to leave. I absolutely do not want to go through that again. It isn't fair at all to me. I have tried my best to get out of this crazy house. I do the exact same thing every single day. There is never any true excitement here. "

"I can understand your pain. I may not know why you are in here but I know that I am in here to recover and I'm not going to have a girl like you stop me from that."

"All you need to know is if you follow the rules that Mary gives then you will be perfectly fine."

"Whatever. This will be a great friendship. I just know it."

When I got settled into the room and everything I went to explore the rest of the house. I wanted to meet the other kids that were there. I found the other girls. They didn't say much, all they did was stare at me. I was hoping it wouldn't be like this the whole time that I was staying there. Then when I went out to the back yard I found the boy. I couldn't believe my eyes. Right there in front of me was Alexander. I ran up to him.

"Alexander. What the heck are you doing here?"

"Julie! Why the heck are you here?"

"I asked you first so now answer."

"I'm here because I have schizophrenia really bad. I got sent here about a year ago. I have been living here ever since."

"When you saw me though you said you lived with your parents. Why did you lie to me?"

"I didn't want you to know the whole truth. I didn't want you to think that I was crazy. I also run away from this place a lot of the times because I don't want to be here. One of the girls covers for me while I'm gone."

"Okay. How in the world has Mary not realized you have been gone? I can't imagine how that is even possible?"

"Like I said one of the girls and I have came up with a plan for whenever I decide to do that. I try to do it only once a week so Mary doesn't become suspicious. Plus Mary doesn't care about me at all. I am crazy."

"Oh wow."

"I thought she would have found out by now but she still has no idea. Please do not ruin it for me."

"I won't. I will let Mary find out by herself."

"Thank you, Julie. You are amazing."

"Thanks. It is almost five so let's go so we won't get yelled at for not being at this meeting."

"You go on, Julie. I will be there in a few minutes. I have to take care of something back here. Don't worry about me. You go because if you aren't on time especially since this will be your first meeting then you will for sure get in trouble."

"Whatever you say, Alexander. Thank you."

When I left Alexander I ran back into the house and went in the living room where everyone was waiting for me. All I got was stares. Just like before. I knew this was going to be a long rest of the evening.

"Come on, Julie, come join the rest of us."

I went and sat down by Hailey, who I was hoping was going to start being nicer to me. I don't think that was going to happen any time soon. When I went and sat down Hailey sort of pushed me and I bumped into the one girl beside me. As soon as that happened everything fell into chaos.

All of the girls got up and started to yell at me. I got scared and started yelling back. Mary then added onto everything by yelling and trying to break everyone apart. It soon led to all of us hitting each other. It got so out of hand that one of the girls accidentally hit Mary in the nose and gave her a nose bleed. When we all noticed that happen we all settled down because we knew we were in some deep trouble. Boy, was I right.

"What the heck were you all thinking? Fighting like this will not be tolerated and you know it!" Mary's face got as red as a fire truck.

The one girl whose name was Allie spoke up. "It is all of Julie's fault. She is the one that bumped into my side on purpose."

"It wasn't on purpose, first of all. I was pushed by Hailey who doesn't like me."

"That is not true, Julie. I adore you."

"Liar, liar, pants on fire."

When I said that Mary got furious. "That is absolutely enough girls. Now everyone go up to their rooms and stay quiet. I don't want to hear another word from anyone until dinner at seven."

We all scurried like squirrels up to our rooms, afraid for what was going to happen at dinner. Alexander should be lucky that he wasn't at the meeting. I was wondering if Mary even noticed that he wasn't there.

Hailey and I didn't even look at each other until dinner. At dinner we were made to sit by each other. We both didn't like that at all. We dealt with it though and got done with dinner without fighting with each other.

That night was weird. After dinner everyone stayed silent and went to do their own things. When we went to bed I had a hard time falling asleep. I kept thinking about everything that happened in the last twenty four hours. I was extremely worried that every single day was going to be like this. I didn't want them to be, but I had a strange feeling about it. Around midnight or so Hailey finally spoke up about the day and night.

Chapter 12

"Julie. Listen. I know we may have gotten off on the wrong path. I am sorry for that. I truly am. I have just went through a lot and am having a hard time coping with it. I lost my parents when I was two years old to a house fire. They sacrificed their lives so I could live. My aunt pulled into my driveway as everything was happening. My aunt was a mess. My parents died instantly. At that point my aunt became my caregiver because she didn't want me to go into the foster care system.

"Three years after that she became a drug addict. One night she got so drunk that she abused me and then took me to a bridge and left me there. I cried for a good three hours. There were so many cars that went past but not one stopped for me in that time period. Luckily, Mary did stop. She was first only going to keep me until the state could find me a new permanent home. A month passed and no luck with a new home so Mary decided to keep me. She officially adopted me when I was seven. I am now thirteen. I try my best to behave but I just can't no matter how hard I try. For that I am sorry."

"Oh, Hailey, I am so sorry to hear all of this. It will get better I can promise you that. I do have a question though. How much do you know about Alexander? I have had a couple instances where I met him and he seems more than a little crazy."

"Yes, he is something else. He has imaginary friends. I believe that he is too old for those childish people of the imagination. but that is just my thinking. I don't talk to him much but I see him talking to something every once in a while."

"Yeah, same here. He says that it follows him everywhere. He also said that if we were to listen carefully we would be able to interact with it just like he can. Even in the dead of silence I haven't been able to hear anything. Of course we have been outside. I thought I heard it once but I didn't."

"Julie, that was in your head. I have never heard anything talk like he claims these 'friends' of his can. Have you met Alexander before? How have you been outside with him when you just arrived here?"

"Yes, I have met Alexander before today. He started following me when I went past his house in New York. He has appeared and disappeared on and off. He finally made up an excuse yesterday to get back here."

"Oh. I didn't know that, Julie. I will make sure Mary knows that he went back to his old house where he isn't allowed to be."

"Why isn't he allowed at his actual parents house?"

"It is a long story. I will tell you in the morning. It is late and we need to get to sleep before Mary comes to check the rooms and sees that we are still up."

"Okay, Hailey. Good night."

"Good night, Julie."

It was about one in the morning after that conversation. I laid in my bed for a little bit longer because I couldn't fall asleep. I had a lot going through my mind. I really wanted tomorrow to be a better day.

That next morning I got up and then something miraculous but still weird happened. Hailey helped me with the morning routine that they usually did. The morning routine was get up, take medication, eat breakfast, do our classes and then the daily chores. All of the kids in the home either were home-schooled or did online classes. I told Mary how I have been doing online classes and she agreed that I could continue to do them as long as I stayed caught up with everything else. If I started to fall behind then she would start teaching me herself. I knew for a fact that I didn't want that so I decided that I was going to try my best to stay caught up in all of my classes. After we were done with classes and our chores we were basically on our own until that evening when our family meeting was. The chores that I had to do were clean up the living room, make my bed, and then put all the clean dishes away. I did those pretty easy because I did all of those things when I was living with my mother.

When I got done with my chores I went upstairs and read for a little bit. I was in the middle of reading "The Sight" by David Clement-Davies. I was right at a good part when Hailey came upstairs and invited me to go swimming with her. It was eighty degrees out and apparently the neighbors had a pool that we could go swimming in. I agreed. Hailey let me borrow one of her swimming suits since I didn't have one yet. It was a really pretty one. It was purple, sparkly, and a two piece. I didn't really have the body for a two piece but I honestly didn't care. Hailey's other swimming suit was a two piece as well. One thing I noticed when we were getting ready were Hailey's arms. They had cuts all over them. I decided to ask her about them.

"Hailey. What is up with your arms?"

"I used to cut but Mary took away everything from me so I couldn't. These are the scars from the last time. I haven't had thoughts for already a month now."

"I'm sorry to hear that you once felt that way. I am here if you ever want to talk about anything. It is great that you aren't having any of those thoughts anymore. Keep it up."

"Thank you, Julie. Let's hurry up. Alexander wanted us to go and swim with him. He also said that this will probably be the last nice day for a while. It is supposed to start getting a lot colder starting tomorrow."

"I would assume since it is technically fall already. I'm surprised it is still this nice outside so I agree with you that we better hurry."

When we got to the pool Alexander was already there. He was teasing us to get in. I was going to jump in but that was before I knew how cold the water was. I wasn't used to the coldness. Before I knew it though Hailey ran up behind me and pushed me into the pool. She jumped in right after. After a couple of hours in the pool Mary called us all in for lunch. When we went in for lunch Alexander disappeared again. He was in the pool when we were called in. I had no idea where he went.

I whispered to Hailey, "Do you know where Alexander went? He was right behind us."

"No I do not. He always does this. He is never here for meals. Since there are so many of us though Mary never notices that he is gone. He always makes sure he is back before we have to meet for our daily family meeting."

"That is so strange."

"Yeah. Let's not talk about it right now so we don't ruin it for him. Let's just eat. Then after this Mary is going to have a couple of us go to the store. I'll see if you and I can go so we can talk more about it."

"Okay, Hailey"

I really didn't want to go with Hailey to the store. I know that we were starting to get along a little better, but I was still uneasy about going anywhere with her. I was hoping that Mary would think the same way and wouldn't make me and Hailey go to the store together. Well, apparently Mary did not think the same way. Hailey and I were the very first ones that she came to and asked if we would be willing to go to the store with each other. I didn't want to seem like I didn't want to go so of course I said yes. Hailey was so happy about that. I think that she really was sorry about the other night and wanted to try her best to be friends with me. I knew that if she was going to try her best then the least that I could do was try my best.

When lunch was done Hailey and I got to go to the store together to get a couple things we needed for dinner. We really didn't talk much like we had planned to, but instead we just chased each other all the way. It was actually a lot of fun. I really didn't expect that at all. Hailey was a lot faster than I was. The reason for that was because she ran in marathons and everything. Apparently she has been running in them ever since she was five years old. I found that interesting about her. I would have never guessed a girl like her would like to run. She barely likes to get up and go downstairs for things. I noticed that today. Right before we went to go swimming she forgot something in the bathroom and she asked me to go get it for her. That is the top notch of laziness in my opinion.

When we got there we walked into the store out of breath. The manager must have known Hailey well because when we got in there she came up and gave Hailey a huge hug. It reminded me a little bit of me and my ex-best friend. Her name was Elizabeth. We used to hug like that whenever we would go an hour without talking or seeing each other. I wish I still had her around at times. The only reason that I didn't was because since my mother used to keep me inside all the time I wasn't be able to go and hang out with Elizabeth anymore.

"I see you have been out running people again. Don't you get sick and tired of that? I would think that you would let other people win at times."

"You know it, Kelly. This is Julie. She will be staying

with me for awhile. She is really nice. You should get to know her sometime."

Kelly gave me a shoulder shrug. It was like she knew me and didn't like me or something. I ignored it. Hailey and I continued getting the things that we needed to get. It took us a lot longer then it should have because we kept messing around. We kept pretending that the fruits were eyes as well as we were making silly faces. We were having so much fun. I don't think Kelly was enjoying it as much. I had a feeling that she wanted us to hurry up and get what we needed so we could get out of there and go home. She kept giving us a really weird look. We then finally decided that we needed to stop and head back home. At the checkout Hailey and Kelly had a little conversation. Hailey kept trying to include me, but then Kelly kept pushing me out of the conversation one way or another. It was rude if you ask me. I quickly ran out of the store while Hailey finished up. I shed a tear or two. Hailey must have known somehow even though I tried not to show it to her that much.

"What's wrong, Julie?"

"I have a weird feeling about Kelly. It seems like she doesn't like me. Didn't you see how she pushed me off and didn't include me in any of the conversations? That kind of hurt. I understand that she has known you a lot longer than she has known me, but it would have been nice if she was nice to me a little bit."

"I understand how you feel, Julie. You have to understand that is how she is. It will take time for her to get used to you. She has known me and the other kids for at least a year. Believe it or not since Alexander is the next in line to the newest kid she still treats him like she treats you."

"Whatever you say, Hailey. Let's hurry up and get going so Mary doesn't get worried and yell at us."

"Okay, Julie."

Of course Hailey and I ran back home. I was surprised that Hailey could still run as fast as she was with grocery bags in both of her hands. This time I was able to keep up with her though. I thought that was incredible. The groceries did slow her down a little bit. When we got home everyone came trampling us because they were hungry. I didn't realize we were gone for as long as we were. I guess we were gone for about two and a half hours. Usually it only takes about an hour according to Mary. She was glad to see Hailey and I getting along with each other. Whether or not I wanted to admit it I was somewhat glad that Hailey and I were getting along as well as we were. When we got home Alexander was mysteriously back. If only we could know where that boy disappeared to all of these time. He didn't talk to us much. He was talking to his voice. We decided to spy on him and try to hear what he was saying.

"Flo. I want to leave this place so badly. I miss my family so much but I know for a fact that they won't take me back. I have lost so much of their trust. Especially my little sisters. I almost lost my family because of what I did. I was so stupid. I wanted to act like I knew everything, but the truth is I don't know everything. I never did and never will. I truly did not mean to hurt them as bad as I did. I should have watched my actions and thought about them before I did anything. If only I had my brother there that day or would have actually went with him like planned none of this would have happened. I also would not be here in this situation that I am in now. It was truly an accident. I let some stupid mistake take over my body which that led to me making bad choices. "

The voice wasn't saying anything back to Alexander. I wish it would just because I don't know what he did to hurt his family. Maybe if the voice would say something back then we would know what happened. Hailey looked at me strangely. We were trying to stay quiet, that way Alexander didn't find out that we were watching him. He started to cry. I knew he thought he was alone with the voice because he would never cry in front of any of us if he knew that we were there. He cried for a couple minutes. He was truly missing his home and family. When he was starting to turn around Hailey and I quickly turned around and ran off before we got caught. I felt so bad for Alexander. I wished that there was something I could do for him so he wouldn't feel so homesick.

"Hailey. Follow me. I need to talk to you in the room before our family meeting."

We ran up to our room.

"What's up, Julie?"

"Do you know anything specific about Alexander's family?"

"No I don't. Why do you ask?"

"I was thinking that maybe we could make something for him so he wouldn't miss his family so much."

"All I know, Julie, is whenever he runs off he goes and tries to go back to his house."

"What happens when he goes?"

"Not sure. He does come home in a more depressed mood than when he left. It is really upsetting to everyone in the house. That is why he is here. He is always really depressed."

"Oh okay. Well I think I have an idea, but I need your help."

"What do you need me to do, Julie?"

"Will you cover for me? I am going to sneak out tonight and go try to find his family to talk to them."

"Are you sure about that Julie? I don't want you to get caught or hurt."

"I will be okay, Hailey. I need to do this for Alexander. If this will help him then I will do it. I care for him a lot and don't want to see him like this. I know what it is like to be depressed and it is not fun at all."

"I understand, Julie. I just don't want to see you get hurt if this doesn't work out."

"I won't. I promise, Hailey. Thank you."

"You're welcome."

That night during the family meeting my mind was occupied of how I was going to escape. I knew that Mary kept all of the doors and windows locked at night. I had no idea how Alexander did it when he ran away. Maybe the voice of his helped him out somehow. The only problem with that is I didn't have a voice friend. I was all on my own on trying to figure out my escape plan. This was harder than I thought it would be. I then came up with the most perfect escape idea. There was nothing that could go wrong with it in my eyes!

My plan would take place that night around eleven when everyone was asleep. That evening was surprisingly calm. Everyone was tired and so we all wanted to get to bed. I had to wait about two hours before I made my first move to execute my plan. When eleven came around Mary still hadn't come to check the rooms so I had to wait even longer until she came and cleared each room. When she finally left my room I quietly got out of bed and snuck downstairs. When I got downstairs I tiptoed around to every door to see if Mary locked all of the doors or not. Luckily she forgot to lock the back door. I was surprised about that. I then opened the door and was on my way.

I had some idea where to go, thanks to the rough guidelines I'd got from staring at Map Quest for an hour. I only had a glimpse of it when trying to stop that fight. It was also completely dark outside with no lights anywhere in sight. This was another thing that was going to bother me. What if Hailey was right about me getting hurt if I didn't get the information that I needed. What if his parents were just as mean as his jerk brother.

It was worth a shot though to try. If I failed I would have to pick myself right back up again and keep trying. I wasn't going to give up. Not for me or Alexander. Alexander needed me to do this. He wouldn't tell me even if I begged him to, but I knew it had to be done.

Chapter 13

I finally did find my way out of the town that I was in. It was easy since I knew the doctors office was right on the edge. It only took me about a half hour to get there. When I was out of the town I just kept going straight, back along the path I'd used to come to the town. It was still completely dark. I kept having thoughts of going back to the house and forgetting about the whole thing. I knew in my mind though that I had to continue. It was for Alexander. He was the only person that was keeping me going. When it was starting to get light out I found that same community garden that I found previously. I decide to try and relax a little before I moved forward. I laid between the flowers and took a little nap.

I slept good for about an hour before I had another one of those bad dreams. This was one of the worst ones yet. This time the snow storm happened but I moved out of the way before the big pile of snow came on me. A couple minutes after the first snow storm there was another one and the same thing happened to me. I woke up screaming my head off. There was no one around to hear me so that was the good thing about that. I knew why it happened too. I forgot to take my medication this morning. I didn't think about grabbing any before I left last night. I really wish I would have though. I hated having these types of dreams. I just wanted to not sleep again until I got back to the house. That way I couldn't have a chance to have those dreams again. I decided to hurry up and find this house so I could talk to Alexander's family. I knew I had to keep focused if I was going to reach my goal. I knew it wasn't impossible. I got up and continued.

By this time it was afternoon and I was so close to the town that the house was at. I needed to retrace my steps to find the house. I knew exactly what the house looked like. I saw Alexander's brother and the girls come out of the house. It was big, black, and shiny. I could definitely tell that his parents were rich. After about another forty minutes of walking I got to the front of the house. I couldn't believe it. I ran up to the door. A lady answered the door.

"Hello. Who are you? May I help you?"

"Hi. Yes my name is Julie. I came to ask you a few questions about your son Alexander. He really misses you guys and I just need to know a few things to help him out."

The lady answered in a rude and mean voice.

"What about Alexander? The little boy almost ruined our family. He is our son but he will never be welcomed back in this house again. Especially after what he did to our daughters!"

"Well that is what I need to know, ma'am. I need to know what he did and why you guys are so mad at him."

"Fine. This is what you need to know. He set the house on fire. He put a match in his sisters' room while they were sleeping. He left the house and went across the street. It only took ten minutes for the whole house to catch on fire. When he saw the house he ran back home and got his sisters and everyone out of the house. He was just in time of getting his sisters out of their room and outside. If he was any later his sisters may or may not have survived. We had to spend thousands of dollars to repair the house back to the way it is now."

"I am so sorry to hear that, ma'am. I had no idea what happened. You know he has came around a couple times to try and see you guys."

"Yes, I am very aware, young lady. Like I tell him every single time, he is not welcomed here anymore. He is the reason that our family is falling apart. Is there anything else you would like to know?"

"Yes. When he was here what were his favorite things?"

"He didn't have any hobbies while he was here. He always got into trouble. He did enjoy a couple things though on those rare occasions when he wasn't in trouble. I have them in a box upstairs if you would like to have that. Either you take them or they go in the trash."

"Yes please."

"Okay, wait right here while I go get them for you."

While I was waiting I looked inside the house for a minute. It was elegant. It for sure did not look like it had any repairs done on it. It didn't even look like a fire had happened. At this point in time I was starting to question if this lady was telling me the truth. I even saw one of his sisters, I think, run past the door and she looked perfectly healthy. I would think that if she was in a fire at all she would have some kind of injuries. Plus the fire couldn't have been that long ago since Alexander has only been with Mary for a year. Right now I didn't believe anything. I didn't say anything though since I didn't want to come out as rude or anything. When the lady came down she dropped the box of things at my feet.

"Here you go. These are all the things that he actually enjoyed and put his time into."

"Well, thank you very much. I am sorry to bother you. Just so you know you are missing out on raising a great guy."

After I said that I hurried up, grabbed the box of stuff and ran as fast as I could. I could hear the lady slam the front door really hard. I felt so bad for yelling at her but it had to be done. If my thinking was right though she wasn't telling me the truth anyways. I knew that I would find out the truth sooner or later. It was light out when I was heading home so maybe I would actually get half way home tonight. By nightfall I found the garden again. I was going to start referring to that garden as my special place because it has always been there for me right when I needed it the most. I climbed right back between the flowers and rested for a little bit. I didn't dare fall asleep though. I was to afraid too.

I only rested for an hour or so. I wanted to get home before morning so Hailey didn't have to keep covering for me. I felt terrible already that I was having her do this for me. It wasn't her responsibility in the first place to cover for my idiotic actions. If Mary found out it would only be my fault and not Hailey's. I knew that if I wasn't home and Mary found out then both Hailey and I would get in trouble. I didn't want that to happen. Especially since Hailey and I were just starting to get along. I didn't want to ruin that.

While I was walking I imagined Alexander again apparently because the voice spoke again. This time it only said one thing to me.

"You better hurry home. Mary is getting ready to get up and do a random bedroom check."

After the voice said that it vanished. I had a strong hatred when it did that. It didn't give me any other information besides that I better hurry up. It would have been great to know how much time I had until she got to my room or something like that. I didn't want to get caught and so on hearing the news that I did I ran. I ran like I would to win a marathon. I couldn't risk anything. I made sure I grabbed the box. That was the only thing that I truly needed. If I got in trouble I wouldn't care as long as I had that box.

It still took me forty minutes to get home even when I was running. When I got there it looked like Allie's light was on so that meant that I had at least fifteen minutes to get up to the room. Allie's room was the first that was checked, then Alexander's, then the other girl's room, and lastly Hailey and I's room. When I tried to go through the back door the same way that I went it was locked. That was my way back in. I went and tried around the house to try and see if there was any other way I could get back in the house and without Mary finding out. While I was walking around the house I heard a voice. It wasn't the voice that comes and goes. This voice was way too familiar. I looked up and saw Hailey. She was trying to tell me something, but I couldn't hear her because she was whispering. She was pointing to the front yard though. I still didn't know what she was trying to say. She then wrote a note to me, crumpled the paper up, and threw it down to me. When I received the note it said:

Go to the front yard. Open the door to the little blue cellar. Go down that. It leads to the basement. I will then help you from there.

I did exactly what Hailey told me to do. When I got to the basement I waited for Hailey to come and get me. If she could really pull this off I was going to owe her a big favor. It took about five minutes for Hailey to get to the basement. When she got there she grabbed my hand quickly and basically dragged me upstairs. When we got to the bedroom she threw me on the bed and told me to go to sleep. That was it for the night. I had a feeling that in the morning I was going to hear it from her.

The bad thing was that since she grabbed my arm so fast and didn't even give me a minute to have a chance to grab the box. The box was still down in the basement just sitting there. I was really hoping that Mary didn't discover that in the morning if she went down there. I decided to forget about it for the rest of the night. I knew that I was going to have a rough day tomorrow. I didn't even want to think about that until the time came. I decided to take the chance and fall asleep.

Chapter 14

I was so right about getting yelled at in the morning. It wasn't by Mary but by Hailey. She was way more than mad, she was furious. Her yell was rambunctious. She made sure she didn't yell too loud so Mary would hear but loud enough that it hurt my ears.

"Julie, yesterday was the last time that I am ever going to cover for you. I almost got in trouble. I had to lie again to Mary because of your dumb decisions. You are the reason that I ended up doing this."

Hailey lifted up her sleeves and then I saw that she harmed herself again.

"Why did you do that, Hailey? Where did you get the things to do it? You didn't have to cover for me. If you would have said no I would have figured something else out to do. Don't you dare blame me for you cutting."

"Whatever, Julie. You are safe and Mary didn't find out."

"Thank you, Hailey."

After that conversation I ran downstairs to get some medicine for Hailey's arm. I had to make sure that Mary didn't see me. I didn't want her to know that Hailey cut herself again. I found some medicine in the downstairs bathroom. I quickly ran up and gave it to Hailey. She refused to take the cream or Band-Aids from me, but I laid them on her bed just in case she changed her mind. I then went downstairs for breakfast.

When I got there everyone including Alexander was there. Alexander looked under the weather though. He didn't touch much of his food either. When he did that I knew something was wrong. Alexander was always hungry no matter what time of day it was. He always ate a lot as well. He did drink some juice, even though I don't know how he could. That stuff was nasty. It smelled like something died in it, I couldn't even drink a half a glass of it. Mary could also tell that he wasn't feeling himself. She let him leave the breakfast table early so he could go up to his room and rest. I had a feeling that is where he was going to be most of the day today. That gave me a great chance to work on my project that I had planned for him.

Which reminded me that the box of his stuff was still on the floor of the basement. I somehow had to get it up to my room without Mary or anyone else seeing me. This was going to be a great challenge. I had a plan though. I asked to use the restroom after I was done with breakfast. Then when I got up, instead of going to the restroom I snuck downstairs to get the box and took it upstairs to my room. It was hard though because the basement door is right behind the kitchen table. Everyone was distracted though by talking about Alexander. By the time I got upstairs everyone was excused from the breakfast table and Hailey was up in the room when I got there.

"What is all of that stuff that you have, Julie."

"It is the box of stuff that Alexander's mom gave me when I was there. It is everything that he liked and enjoyed doing while he was there. She made it clear though that he is never welcomed back into that house. Even though I don't think she is telling the truth of what really happened. I think she was making it up to get me away from there."

"Well what are we waiting for? Let's jump into searching this thing. What is your idea exactly, Julie?"

"I was planning on doing like an artist canvas of a collage of everything in here. That way when he looks at it he will have happy thoughts and not depressing ones. What do you think of that idea, Hailey?"

"I think that is a great idea. Can I help with it?"

"Of course you can, Hailey. I just have to figure out how to make it first."

"Okay, Julie. Please let me know when you need me."

As soon as Hailey left the room I went to brainstorm ideas. This was going to be fun. Before I started though I decided to go and check on Alexander to see if he was feeling any better. When I got to his bedroom door I tried to enter but it was locked. That was strange because we aren't allowed to have our doors locked at any time. I tried to bang on the door to get him to answer but he wouldn't come open up the door. I finally decided to use my nail and try to break the lock so I could get in. It took me a few minutes but I finally got in. When I got in I couldn't find Alexander anywhere. I looked all around. I did find another note that was laying on his bed. I was getting used to finding these notes. This one said:

I absolutely hate it here. It is torture. I am thankful that Mary brought me into the home a year ago, but it is starting to get to be way too much. The rules here are way too strict. I can't keep up with day to day activities and chores. I wish life was a lot more simpler. To top it all off I have a hopeless crush on a girl that is here. She doesn't know it, but even if she did know it she wouldn't feel the same way. I just know it. Oh well, it is what it is. I just don't want to be here anymore. If anyone finds this note please don't come looking for me. I want to be alone. Thank you very much. I am so sorry that I am just a huge disappointment to all of you guys. I promise I will try and be better.

I couldn't believe what I just read. I never knew this is how Alexander really felt. I didn't think living here was that bad either. I mean I knew that it could be hard sometimes and that Mary had some strict rules and guidelines, but it was all for the safety and health of us kids. Mary only wants what is best for us. He was also definitely not a disappointment. I knew that from the way everyone treated him. They all treated him like a brother. From the minute I saw Amanda and Hailey work with Alexander to get a chore done when he was struggling, to when Allie was right there beside him when he just needed a shoulder to cry on. I knew that he was put here for a specific reason. That statement in his letter was so not true.

I also knew that the girl that he had a crush on was me. He was right that I didn't feel the same way about him. I couldn't. I also didn't want to feel the same way. Even if I did I didn't want to be in a relationship. They don't always work out for me.

Anyways, I knew I had to go and find him. Even though his note said he wanted to be left alone, I wanted to go find him and bring him back to where he belonged. I did care about him and didn't want to see him hurt. This time I didn't tell Hailey where I was going or why. I didn't want her to freak out and then feel like she has to lie to Mary again and then that wouldn't lead to her hurting herself. I think I knew exactly where Alexander was.

I snuck out of the house and headed to where Alexander found me by the garden. I knew that would be the place he was because that was the place that he snuck into my sleeping bag. Since I knew that I was the girl that he liked that would be the place he was. It meant something special to him. Luckily the garden wasn't that far from the edge of the town. It only took me forty minutes to get there. The garden was there, but I couldn't find Alexander anywhere.

It took me a while to find him, but I finally found him. He was higher up in the tree that was there. I didn't even realize that the tree was that high. He was sleeping, it looked like to me and I knew I wouldn't be able to climb that high to wake him up. I then did the one thing I knew I could do. I yelled. As soon as I yelled it scared Alexander so badly that he fell out of the tree and hit the ground. I ran over to him so fast to make sure that he was okay.

"Are you okay, Alexander? I didn't mean to have you fall."

He wouldn't answer me. I got scared.

"Alexander. Please answer me. Don't scare me like this."

Alexander did open his eyes. His gorgeous eyes. That was a relief.

"Julie? Is that you?"

"Yes, Alexander, it is me."

"How did you find me?"

"I came to the one place I knew you would be. I found your note and I know that I am the girl that you have a crush on. You were right that I just don't feel the same way about you. I do care about you though and so I came to make sure you were okay and to take you back home. Please listen to me and come back home. We both know that is the place that you need to be. Even though you will deny it, deep down you know that it is the right thing for you."

"I don't want to go back home though. Did you not understand what I said in my letter? It is not the right place for me. You will eventually find the same exact thing out. It is only a matter of time. You have only been there for a couple of days so of course you are going to think that the home is perfect. Well, let me tell you one thing, Julie. It is not perfect. It never was and never will be."

"I did understand, but I know that you would be a lot safer if you were at home with people who care and love you. I can see that you may not think we do but please understand that we do. We would do anything to see you happy. What do you mean by it isn't the right place for you? Mary seems so nice. All the girls there care deeply about you. I know that for a fact."

"Whatever you say, Julie, but I am not coming home. Mary can be really nice at times, but before you came me and her had some of our own troubles. She used to beat me and make me stay in the basement for days on end. She would make sure I was fed and everything, but she wouldn't let me come upstairs. She thought that I was a threat to all of the other girls. The only reason she is keeping me is because she is getting money from the state to keep me there. She gets money for keeping us all there. It is mandatory I guess. "

"Okay, I can understand where you are coming from about Mary, but I doubt that all of what you are saying is true. I can never see Mary being that mean to you or any of us in that matter. I do know that she is getting money from the state. This is her job. Her job is to take care of all of us. How else is she supposed to get the money if someone doesn't pay her? I don't care how much you don't want to come back home. If you won't listen to me then you gave me no choice."

I grabbed Alexander by the arm and I started to drag him. He was starting to resist, but I was stronger than him so I could handle him. It took me twice as long to get home. When I got home I didn't even think about sneaking back inside the house so I wouldn't get caught. I just wanted to get Alexander inside the house and back up to his bed where he belonged. I was going to make sure Mary knew everything as well. I didn't care if I got in trouble. Alexander's safety and health were the number one important things to me.

When I walked in Mary was right there in front of the door. She didn't yell at me at first, instead she just gave Alexander and I a hug, making sure that we knew she was happy that we were home and safe. If Alexander didn't think that was a sign of how much Mary cared about us then I don't know what would show him. The whole rest of the night was awkward between everyone in the house. I felt so bad, but I figured that Mary would eventually talk to both Alexander and I to find out what in the world happened with us.

I was correct about that. That night before bed Mary came up to talk to me. Surprisingly she wasn't yelling, she was calm about the whole entire thing, She sat on the edge of my bed. "What happened, Julie? Where did you go today? I was worried sick about you and Alexander."

"I went to go find Alexander. I found a note on his bed today. He said that he didn't want to be found, but I care about him way too much and wanted him here with the people that care about him. I also didn't want him to do something that he would regret. I knew if he was out there any longer that there was a good chance of something happening. "

"Well, I really appreciate that, Julie. You have no idea how much that means to me. You are not in trouble this time. Next time though, will you please let me know before you go and try to find someone. I want to make sure you are safe as well."

"Okay, Mary. I will, I promise. Thank you so much, Mary."

"You are welcome. Now here, take your meds and try to get some sleep. I will talk to Alexander in the morning when he is feeling better."

"Okay."

As soon as Mary left I laid down and tried to get some sleep. I was exhausted after the long day that I had to deal with. It was really hard for me. I kept thinking about what would've happened if I didn't go find Alexander. Would he still be there in the tree? I also probably wouldn't have gotten talked to. If I didn't do anything though the house would just feel incomplete. There would be a part of me missing. If I was being honest to myself Alexander was my first true friend. He was the one that helped me eat and not starve myself. I was truly thinking that he was the main reason that I wanted to ask for help. I owed him a huge thanks.

Chapter 15

The next morning went just like any other except that Alexander was still not feeling well. He didn't even come down for breakfast. That was really strange even for Alexander. Mary told everyone that Alexander was probably going to end up going to the hospital after breakfast. Everyone started to freak out. Mary tried to get everyone to get quiet, but that didn't work the way that she had planned. I was the first one to get down from the table and run up the stairs to Alexander's room. I quickly went into the room and got down beside his bed making sure that he was okay. He looked really sick. He was pale, had cold hands, sweaty palms, high temperature, and barely breathing. I started freaking out. I didn't want to lose my best friend. Mary came running upstairs and pulled me out of the room. She told me that his room was off limits as of now. The only person that was allowed in his room was her. It wasn't fair. I wanted to be right there beside him. I ran into my room crying. Hailey came in and tried to calm me down a little bit.

"Julie. Everything will be okay. Alexander will be okay as well. Mary will be taking him to the doctors and they will make sure he is alright. They will do everything in their power to get him feeling better."

"How do you know that, Hailey? What if he is really sick and they don't have any medicine to help him get better?"

"They will, Julie. You just have to keep the faith and pray about it."

"Why though? That won't do anything to help him get better."

"Prayer always works, Julie. Trust me. Prayer is the only thing that keeps me going most days."

"Whatever you say, Hailey. I guess I will try that one day."

"Good. It really does work."

After Hailey and I were done talking, Mary came into the room and told us that she was calling an ambulance to come and get Alexander because she didn't think she would be able to get him to the hospital. I started to get really worried. I didn't think that Alexander was so sick that it was to a point where he had to go the hospital. When Mary told us all about Alexander that morning I was in so much disbelief. Now that Mary was actually calling an ambulance I was starting to believe it a lot more. We all waited patiently with Alexander. It only took the ambulance five minutes to get to the house. That was a record time I think. Every time I would have to call the ambulance in the past it would take them more than ten minutes. As soon as the ambulance came they took Alexander and he was off. Mary went along with him. We were all left at the house and given chores to do. I did the chores that Alexander usually did so that they would get done. I tried not to break down crying, but I couldn't hold it in. Hailey was there to comfort me though.

That evening around dinner time Mary was still not home from the hospital so the one girl Allie decided to cook dinner for everyone. She made chicken, homemade apple sauce, and green beans. It was delicious. I definitely could not cook as well as she could. No one knew that Allie could cook. Let alone cook for four girls. After dinner we all went to do our nightly routine. Right before we went to bed Mary came home from the hospital. Alexander wasn't with her though.

"Girls, I have some news to tell you guys."

"What is it, Mary?" Allie asked.

"The doctors told me that Alexander is very sick. They are going to be doing some tests tonight to see if there is anything they can do to help him not get sick as much. They did say that he would have to stay for a week. The doctor also mentioned that whatever he has is not contagious. He was born with it as it is a genetic disease. That is meaning his parents have whatever he has. It just took seventeen years to catch up to him."

"No! This isn't fair one bit. Why did it have to happen to him? It should of happened to me!" I yelled.

I then ran up to my room crying. Everyone else just stayed in the living room shocked. No one spoke for at least the next hour. We all just wanted this to be a dream and wanted to wake up and Alexander to be okay and be able to come home first thing tomorrow morning. That night Hailey came up and right before bed she knelt down at her bed to pray. Even though she didn't say anything out loud I knew exactly what she was doing. My dad used to take me to church when I was younger. I just couldn't and didn't believe in God at the time. I did take what Hailey told me into consideration. Maybe she was right, and prayer does really work. When Hailey went to bed I knelt down and prayed.

"Dear God, I just want to come and pray to you that you help Alexander get better and soon. I pray that you give the nurses and doctors the wisdom that is needed. I also pray that you give us all here at home the patience that is needed. I hope you can accept this. I know I haven't prayed since I was young. Lord, I am sorry for that. I hope I can get better at praying to you. Thank you, Lord. I also want to thank you for everything that you have blessed me with. I know this isn't the most perfect situation that I am in, but it is a situation that you put me in and for the best. Thank you again, Lord."

After I prayed I quietly got into bed hoping that Hailey was right when she said that prayer really does work. She told me that in all seriousness. I wanted to try and believe what she said. All I wanted, or in this case what everyone wanted, was for Alexander to get better and be right back at home where he belongs. That night I took my medicine that way I could sleep peacefully. That night I didn't have a bad dream but I had a weird one.

The dream was where Alexander and I were dating. It was really fun though. Definitely not what I would have in mind if Alexander and I did end up dating. It was like we were the perfect couple. In my dream we never argued with each other, always held hands, supported each other, were always there for one another, and lastly he was a excellent kisser.

That is what woke me up. I didn't want to dream about that. Even though after I woke up I felt like it was real and it was meant to be. I didn't know if my dream was trying to tell me something or not. Maybe I could possibly take it into consideration if Alexander got better. That was a big maybe though. I for sure knew that I wasn't ready for a relationship. Not yet at least. I don't think I was stable enough to be able to properly function in a relationship. I was really hoping that Alexander would see and understand that. I wanted to try and finish up my treatment and get out of this house and on my own before I even thought about a relationship. If I didn't finish my medication then I could all of a sudden have another mental breakdown. Then who knows what in the world could happen. I could hurt someone and not mean it. By someone I mean Alexander. I couldn't risk any of that.

I needed some serious sleep. My medication was starting to kick in so I started to fall back asleep. That meant my mind was shutting down on me. I went back to sleep and started dreaming the same dream again. It was peaceful. I was starting to wish that Alexander was here with me.

Chapter 16

The next couple of days went slowly. None of us wanted to do anything. All we wanted to do was go to the hospital and see Alexander. We also wanted to make sure that there was nothing that he needed from us. We were strictly told by Mary though that we were not to be at the hospital at all. Alexander needed his rest. It was stressful at home without him.

The only good thing about him not being at the house was that I could work on my project for him without having to worry about him finding it. I decided that I could get it done by the time he was able to come home so that way it would be in his room already and it would be a huge surprise. I spent over twenty hours on it. Hailey helped me a lot. She did a bunch of the gathering, cutting of pictures out of magazines and old books that were in the box of Alexander's, and the border of the poster. After it was done it had a huge guitar painted on it, a few race cars pasted on, book titles on it, and finally it had in big bold letters **Alexander's Favorite Activities.** When I showed Mary she helped me hang it up in his room. It looked amazing. I then decided to write him a note as well.

Alexander, I hope you like what Hailey and I created for you. I know you are probably going to be wondering how I knew what all of your favorite things were. Well, I am going to tell you the whole story right now. I decided one day to go to your parents house and try to figure out what happened. Hailey and I overheard you talking to your imaginary friend. We didn't want you to know that we were watching you. Well, then I wanted to do something to help you. When I went to your parents house your mom told me some story that I do not believe. She then gave me a box of your stuff that you enjoyed the most when you were living there. I had to come up with an idea of how to involve some or all of the things in a project for you. I really hope you enjoy. Maybe if you get better and want to try to date I think I would like that idea. I hope you feel better soon. I love and care about you Alexander.

Sincerely,

Julie

That evening Mary came home with some very exciting news. She told us that the doctors said Alexander could come home in the next day or two. He would have to be on bed rest basically, but he could come home. Everyone got really excited when we heard that news. We spent the next two days cleaning and preparing the house like crazy. We wanted everything to be perfect for the homecoming of Alexander. He deserved all the best, especially from the people who care about him the most. I think I was the most excited for him to return. I wanted him to read the note so he knew what it was like when he wasn't here with me, in my arms. Without him here half of my heart was not here with me. Everybody else was excited but not as excited as I was. I needed my boy home with me. I knew he would want to be with me. We both wanted to be together and that's all that really mattered to me.

The night before he came home I laid in bed thinking about what Alexander's reaction would be when he read that note saying that I wanted to be with him. When Hailey realized that I wasn't asleep she came over and wanted to talk to me.

"What's wrong, Julie? Are you okay? We should be sleeping."

"I know, Hailey. It is just I wrote a letter to Alexander and said that I liked him and if he wanted to date then I would love to try to date."

"No you did not, Julie!"

"Yes I did. He was the first one to admit to me that he liked me."

"That is not right, Julie. Mary is going to freak out if she ever finds out."

"Why? It isn't like Alexander and I are actually brother and sister."

"No but Mary doesn't and won't allow anyone to date while we are here. She is making us wait until we are out of the house. That way she knows that we will be stable and be able to handle relationships in life on our own."

"I can understand that but I really don't care. If Alexander and I decide to date then that is on us. Not you. I won't get you involved and if we get in trouble then let us. It will be totally worth it. Also I'm not even saying that we are going to be dating. It is only if Alexander is wanting to. We shall see."

"Whatever you say, Julie. Whatever you do you better not get me involved. I will not do anything like that again. I want to get out of this house as soon as I can. As long as I finish up my medication and behave within the next five years and don't end up back where I started then I will be out of here and on my way to an amazing life style."

"You will do great at achieving that, Hailey."

"Well, thank you, Julie. I am done talking to you about all of this. It is late and we need to go to sleep. We need to be up early tomorrow to do some last minute things around the house for Alexander to get home in the afternoon after lunch."

That next morning I was the very first one up. Mary left us a note saying that she was at the hospital with Alexander helping him get ready to come home. In the note she mentioned that there was pancake mix in the cabinet for someone to make everyone. I was phenomenal at making pancakes so I started to make them. They must have smelled good because by the time they were done all of the rest of the girls were up, downstairs, and at the breakfast table ready to eat. I was shocked. I didn't realize that I could make the pancakes smell that good. I got everyone served food and we sat down and enjoyed the breakfast. We all talked about how it wasn't the same without Alexander and how we couldn't wait to have him back home with us.

After breakfast we all got up to start finishing cleaning the house. I went and cleaned Alexander's room. It was disastrous. I didn't think that a room could be this messy. He had all of his dirty clothes all over the floor, the bed wasn't made, he had old nasty food all over, and last but not least it smelled like something had died in there. I wouldn't be surprised at all if that was true. It was going to take me forever to finish cleaning this thing called a room. I couldn't even imagine how this boy could sleep in here when he was home. The bed was the first thing I started to clean. I was determined to get this done for Alexander. That was the only thing that was keeping me motivated.

The next three hours I was working like never before. I finally did get it done. When I finished it looked like no one has even slept in the bedroom before. The bed was made, the old food was thrown away outside, and all of the dirty clothes were either thrown in the dirty laundry basket or they were washed. It looked amazing if you were to ask me. I couldn't believe that I got it done. I was proud of myself.

Right after I got finished with the room Mary called the house. She said that she would be on her way home with Alexander in a half hour. Everyone got excited. We all decided to make a sign for Alexander. Since we only had a little bit of time to get it done we all worked together. With all of the girls working on it we got it done in about twenty minutes. It said **Welcome Home Alexander! We Love You!** When we heard the car door we all got into our positions. We held the banner so that way the first thing that Alexander saw when he walked through the door was the banner and all of our smiling faces. We heard the door opening and started squirming because we were just that excited that he was finally able to come home. When that door opened his face lit up. He acted like a kid that just got adopted and was coming into their new home for the very first time.

He ran up to all of this and gave us each a hug. I was last, but he gave me the longest hug. It felt amazing when he did that. His hugs were the one thing that I missed the most. Right before he let go of me he sneaked a kiss on my check. He told me that Mary brought me the note that I left on his bed this morning. He said that he read it and that he would love to try and date. When he told me that I was even more happier. I couldn't show it though since Mary would never allow us to date. So we had to try and keep it a secret from everyone. To show my excitement I ran outside and yelled at the top of my lungs. I was so happy.

That evening at dinner Alexander gave me another big hug because he knew that I was the one that cleaned his room. He really liked the big art project that Hailey and I created for him. I knew that he would like it. I knew that this relationship would be a great thing. The only hard thing was going to be keeping it from everyone. Half of me thought that was the best idea, but then the other half of me wanted everyone in the world to know that Alexander and I were dating. I slept peacefully that night. I had a fabulous dream.

The dream was about Alexander again. At this time we had been dating for about a year already. We were on a nice picnic at the park. We were just laying on a blanket looking up to the stars. He had his arm around me and we were cuddling together. It felt like nothing before. I didn't want it to stop. I was really wishing that it wasn't a dream and that it was reality. It felt so real though. When all of a sudden I felt a jerk that pulled me out of bed. It was Alexander.

He grabbed me and pulled me out of my room and into his. He made sure that I was going to be quiet by covering my mouth. I wanted to slap that boy so much. I had no idea what was going through his crazy mind when he was doing it. If Mary or Hailey would of heard either of us then me and him both would get in so much trouble. When we got into his room he quickly shut the door. He didn't say anything, but he did kiss me. It felt good. Then he led me to his window. He opened the window and pointed out to something far in the distance. I couldn't quite figure out what it was. I squinted really hard and then I knew exactly what it was. It was the tree in the garden. Something was different about it though. That is when it hit me.

The tree was decorated in my favorite color. Pink that was.

"Do you want to go see it closer, Julie? You can see something from the very top of it."

"Sure, but I don't want to get into any trouble."

"We won't get in trouble, Julie. I can promise you that. It will only take us an hour and a half at the most. It is twelve thirty now and we will leave at one, that way we leave after Mary has came around and checked to make sure all of us are in bed and are asleep. Your room is the last one she checks, as soon as she leaves just sneak over here and knock on my door twice so I can let you in. Do you understand, Julie?"

"Yes, I understand, Alexander." I gave him a quick kiss before I left to go back into my room.

When Mary came into the room to check on everyone I pretended that I was sleeping that way I didn't get caught not sleeping. As soon as she left I quickly and quietly tiptoed to the door and waited until Mary walked into her room. As soon as her door shut I went to Alexander's room. I did exactly what he told me to do and he opened up the door. We then snuck out the window and started to head to what I am going to start calling "our tree." I would always remember the tree. It would always have a special place in my heart.

Alexander and I held hands all the way to the tree. When we got there I couldn't believe my eyes. The tree was decorated all fancy. It seemed like Alexander wanted to impress me more then he already has. I can't even imagine how much work he must have put into decorating that tree. It had pink cloth, pink and purple lighting, and lastly it had sparkles all over. He then grabbed me again and lead me up the tree. It was difficult for me to get up there since I wasn't that good of a climber. Alexander had to help me get up.

When we got up there though I saw the most beautiful thing ever. They were the Twin Towers in New York City. I only lived forty minutes away from there at my old place, but I have never visited them in person. I couldn't see them either from where I used to live. The Twin Towers were so impressive. It was unimaginable. They were all lit up.

"So how do you like the Twin Towers, Julie?"

"They are awesome."

"That is what I thought. I try to come up here at least twice a week to see them all lit up and everything. They look brand new still even though they have been there for twenty odd years. I always leave at one after the nightly check."

"That is outstanding, Alexander. We better get going now. I am actually really tired and want to get some sleep before tomorrow. I have a doctor's appointment tomorrow to get a refill on my medication and to check up on how I am doing. I also want to try and search for a job. Believe it or not I want to get out of the house as soon as I possibly can."

"Okay, Julie. We can head home. Before we do come closer."

When I did that me and Alexander cuddled for a couple minutes. After that I didn't say a word to him. I was too shocked of what just happened. We quietly walked back home hand in hand. When we got back home we both quietly snuck back in and went to our rooms. I went right to sleep and had another peaceful night's sleep. I was hoping that what happened this morning could and would happen more often.

Chapter 17

The next morning I slept in even though I didn't mean to. I actually wanted to be the first one up so I could get all ready for my doctor's appointment. Mary had to get me up though when I wasn't up by ten. I then ate breakfast and hung out with a couple of the other girls before I left. I got to know Amanda a little bit. She was really cool, shy, funny, intelligent, and caring. She is the only other girl except for Hailey that has been in the house for eight years. That is all she would basically tell me.

I didn't really want to go to my appointment, but I knew it was necessary. If I didn't go then there was more of a chance then I would be in this house much longer than I wanted to be. Even though if I left the house I would miss Alexander a lot. If this relationship did work out without anyone finding out. Maybe if all worked out though he would be out on his own as well and we wouldn't be able to keep the relationship from everyone anymore. That would be fantastic if that could happen. I ended up going to my appointment.

When I got there I had to wait more than an hour to see my therapist. I hated waiting this long. I thought the point of calling and making an appointment was so I wouldn't have to wait long when I got here. When I get back there my original therapist wasn't there, but a new one was there. I got so frustrated.

"Where is Dr. Ramirez? I want my therapist. I won't talk to anyone else unless it is Dr. Ramirez."

"Well, I am sorry, Julie. I am Dr. Ramone. Dr. Ramirez is really sick today and so I am filling in for her. She told me everything that I need to know about you. She told me to record our session so she could hear everything when she came back into the office. Now I would appreciate if you would just work with me so we both can get our jobs done."

"Well then you both are going to have a really hard time getting me to say anything 'cause it is not happening. I don't care how much you want me to. I don't trust you and I only trust Dr. Ramirez. I will not help you get what you need done."

"Well then, Julie, I see how it is. I guess you just want to be in that home for another year."

"I couldn't care less. I love that home. That is the first place that I have been in the past three years that I have actually felt like people care and love me. They are always nice to me and they will actually help me through all of my problems."

"That is great news, Julie. Anything else you would like to tell me? I see that you have finished the first batch of your medication. How do you feel about that?"

"I am not telling you anything else. Yes, I have finished my medication and need a refill. I want to be on my way to living on my own. I am going out and looking for a job later today. If you can just please refill my prescription and I will be on my way."

"Okay, Julie. We made some good progress. Dr. Ramirez has on this sheet that she wants you to come back in two weeks from today."

"Will do. Thank you Dr. Ramone. I am sorry that I was being rude earlier. I just wanted my own therapist. You did help me a lot. "

As soon as Dr. Ramone wrote my prescription I ran out of that office as fast as I possibly could. I couldn't stand being there anymore. I couldn't wait until Dr. Ramirez was back. I was going to do what I told Dr. Ramone. I was going to go and actually try and find a job.

I went into the little village and there I actually found a couple places that had signs that said "**Help Wanted**". Even though there were many places that needed help I just didn't know which one to apply to. I didn't find any place that fit my interest. It wasn't until I got twenty minutes into the village when I saw this mini art studio. I thought to myself that this would be the perfect place for me to work. I walked into the place and my mind was blown. It was like what I always dreamed an art studio would be. It had famous art pictures hung up on all four walls. There was a man at the front desk. He looked very familiar I just couldn't figure out where he was from.

"Hi. I am here to apply for a job."

"Welcome. We are in desperate need for workers. You don't need to have any specific qualifications or experience, you just have to have a passion for art. I have an application you can fill out right here. If you want you can fill it out here or you can take it home and then bring it back in whenever it is convenient for you."

"I have time to fill it out now. I am going to say that I have a huge passion for artwork."

"Okay, great. You can sit over there."

The man handed me papers that I needed to fill out. It was hard to fill out because I didn't know any of my information like my social security or the address of the group home. I gave him the name of the group home and put on the application that I would bring him that information in the next few days whenever I had that information. When I handed him the papers back he looked it over.

"I will look this information over and give you a call back."

"Sounds good."

"My name is Mr. Popas, by the way."

"Nice to meet you."

I went back to the house to tell everyone about how I might have a job in the next couple of days. Everyone was so happy when all of a sudden I got a phone call.

"Hello?"

"Is this Julie?"

"Yes, it is."

"This is Mr. Popas. I wanted to let you know that I looked over your application and I am pleased to announce that I would like to have you as an employee at my art studio."

"Really?"

"Yes, really."

"Thank you so much."

"You're welcome. You can start tomorrow at eleven. If you can bring in the information that you were missing from the application."

"You got it. I will be there on time."

After that conversation I told everyone the good news. Mary was the most excited about it.

"That is great, Julie. I am so happy for you. You are on your way to being able to live on your own. You just have to keep a job for at least six months and be able to afford to keep an apartment."

"Yes. Thank you so much, Mary, for everything you have done for me. I don't know where I would be without you. The person at the art studio though seemed familiar, but I just couldn't put my finger on it."

"I am sure you will find out sooner or later."

That night I went to bed. I just couldn't wait to start my new journey.

Chapter 18

The next morning I was so excited to start my new job. I got up before anyone else so I could spend extra time to get ready. I wanted to try my best to impress my new boss. I still couldn't think or remember where he was from. I really wish that I could. Oh well, I didn't really care, it wasn't even all that important to me. I guess I made a lot of noise because Mary came down asking what in the world I was doing up making so much noise.

"I am so sorry, Mary. I am just really excited to start my new job today. I have to be there in the next hour. I don't want to leave a bad impression for him. Especially since I could possibly know him I just don't know it yet."

"It is alright, Julie. Just calm down and slow down. You will be just fine. I know it. You are an amazing lady and this is the perfect job for you. Now go brush your teeth and then I will curl your hair for you."

"Thank you again, Mary."

I gave Mary a hug and went and did exactly what she told me. When she did my hair it turned out perfectly. I didn't know that Mary could do hair this good. It looked flawless. My hair was such a mess before she did it. After she was done there were no tangles and it was so smooth. By the time it was done I had a half hour to get to the studio. I ran there.

When I got there I was out of breath. Before I walked in I stopped and caught my breath so my boss didn't know that I ran there. I was greeted by a new person. This person was an older lady.

"Hi. I am here to start my first day. I talked with a gentleman yesterday."

"Hi. You must be Julie. I am Mrs. Capes. You spoke with Mr. Popas yesterday. He is in his office. If you go straight back here down this hall and then take a left, his office will be on the right. Welcome, Julie. I know that you will find this place to be just what you have imagined it to be."

"Well thank you, Mrs. Capes."

When I went to meet Mr. Popas in his office he wasn't there, but his door was open. I just went to sit down in a chair and waited patiently for him. His office had pictures of his family. It was him, his wife, two daughters, and a son. They also had three dogs. It looked like the dogs were a German Shepherd, a Golden Retriever, and a Bulldog. It looked like the perfect family. I was looking at one of his pictures when he suddenly walked in and scared the life out of me.

"Hi, Julie. I am glad that you could make it. Thanks for taking interest in my pictures of my new family. I just recently got married to my wife Ashley. We have liked each other for a couple years but situations happened to where we couldn't be together. Then when we were finally able to be together we dated for a couple months and then we got married. Those are her three children. Their names are Sophia, Annaliese and Matthew. They are amazing children."

"They look like they are amazing. Do you have any other children from your previous marriage."

Mr. Popas didn't answer that question. I just assumed that he didn't want to talk about that. I just changed the topic.

"What will I be doing here?'

"You will mostly be taking phone calls, taking orders for paintings, making orders for new supplies, and last but not least you will be hanging up new paintings whenever someone comes in and buys a painting. Do you understand, Julie?"

He put his head down after he said my name. I knew something was up, just didn't know what it could be yet.

"Yes, I understand, Mr. Popas."

"Good. First you will be doing inventory. Follow me and I will take you to the back where we keep all of the supplies."

When we got to the back room it was filled with supplies. I imagine this would be an artist's dream world if they could have all of this.

"Now, Julie. There is a list here of how many packages or gallons of paint that we need. Then after you are done with this you will be calling different places and making orders. That way we can stay on top of things and we make sure we never run out of supplies."

"Okay. I will get started right away."

"Thank you, Julie. You will work eight hours on the weekends and five hours on weekdays. We have your schedule that way so when you start back up at school you can still do good in school while you are working. Since today is a Saturday you will be working until seven tonight. You will get a lunch break at two. You will get forty five minutes on weekends and thirty minutes on weekdays."

"I got it. Now may I please get started, Mr. Popas? I am very excited to start."

"Go right ahead then, Julie. I am glad to have you working here."

As soon as Mr. Popas left I started to count all of the supplies. To be honest it was pretty boring, but I couldn't complain since I had a job. I was just blessed beyond belief that I found this job. I felt like this was going to turn into something great.

When two came around I was so close to being done counting the supplies, I honestly didn't want to take my break. When Mr. Popas came in he made me go eat lunch. He said that it was mandatory that I went on break. Reluctantly I listened. Since I had forty five minutes for break I was allowed to go home for lunch.

When I got home everyone wanted to hear how my first day was going so far.

"Well everyone, it is going pretty good. It is a little boring, but that is just because I am doing inventory today. Then after I get done with that if we are in need of anymore supplies I will be making calls to order more. It sounds like we will never be running out of supplies. If we are low on supplies then I am told to mark it down so I can order more. I only have forty five minutes of a break today. Then on the weekdays I will only get thirty minutes. That is to ensure that I get off in enough time so I can get home and get homework done. That really won't matter to me as I am just staying with online classes. That is what is most helping me."

"That sounds good to me, Julie." Mary said. "Well you better get some food quickly before you have to head back to work. I made some fish for lunch. There is still some in the fridge for you. I had to stop Allie from eating it all because she loves how I cook the fish. She decided that she was going to be nice and save you some."

"Thank you, Allie. That was nice of you."

"You are welcome, Julie. It was hard, but I managed."

We all laughed after Allie said that. I then quickly heated up some fish and ate. By the time I was done eating I only had about fifteen more minutes to get back to the studio. I grabbed my coat and I was out the door. I was in such a rush that I forgot to shut the door. The only way I knew that is because I heard Alexander yell, "Next time shut the door behind you, loser!"

"Whatever you say!"

I got to the studio right on time. No one was in the office when I got there. There was a sign that said "**Thirty minute lunch break.**" I took the sign down since I was back in the office. I was hoping no one came into the studio to buy any paintings. If they did then I would have no idea of what to do.

It was just my luck that someone did come into the store.

"Hi. I am here to pick up an order."

"What is the name?"

"Nolan."

"Okay, if you wait right here, ma'am, I will try and go see if I can find it. I am new here and don't know where everything is at yet. I think I have an idea though. So if you wait right here I will be right back."

"Take your time, dear. I am a couple minutes early anyways."

I went into the room that was right beside the office. I thought that is where I saw all of the paintings at. When I got in there I started to look around. I realized that all of the paintings were in alphabetical order. That was just amazing for me. I went until I found Nolan. I came out with the painting. It was of a city landscape.

"Is this it, ma'am?"

"Yes it is, young lady."

The price tag was right on the picture. I went to the cash register to try and see if I could finish this order for this lady. The instructions were on the cash register. So I just followed what it said.

"That will be two hundred and fifty dollars."

The lady handed me the money. I carefully put it in the cash register.

"Have a nice day, ma'am."

"You too, young lady."

I couldn't believe that I did that all by myself. I really wished someone was there to see it all go down. I was so proud of myself. Little did I know Mr. Popas and the older lady were watching me from outside. I didn't know that until I was about to go home. Mr. Popas stopped me right before I walked out the door.

"Julie. You did amazing earlier today when getting Mrs. Nolan her picture. The amazing thing was that I haven't even trained you on the cash register yet. I also didn't show you where we kept all of the orders at. How in the world did you figure all of that out?"

"I just followed the instructions on the cash register. For the picture I just used common sense. There is only one other room in the studio beside your office and the back room. I just assumed that was where the pictures were at. I assumed correctly."

"Well, great job. You also did an amazing job making calls to order more supplies. You are a fast learner. You remind me of someone that I love dearly."

"Who would that be, Mr. Popas?"

"I would rather not talk about it."

"Okay, that is fine. I won't ask again. When should I come in tomorrow?"

"I want you to come back here at noon."

"Okay."

As soon as I left I ran home. I was so exhausted. It was a great first day. I didn't think that I would love working as much as I do. I knew that working here for six months was going to be easy. Especially if my boss and the receptionist lady were as nice as they were today.

When I got home everyone was in the living room. They pushed our family meeting back just so I could be a part of it. I thought that was nice of them to do that. During the meeting Mary discussed what would be happening in the next couple of months. She said that we will be getting a couple more kids. These kids were going to be younger. She also said that we were going to have to start doing our school work a lot more and that we can't be slacking. The reason for this was because even though we all were either home-schooled or took online classes we all were going to be having to take an exam to be able to either move to the next grade or graduate. I was the only one that would be able to graduate. As soon as we all heard this we groaned and sighed. We didn't like the idea at all. After the family meeting we were all told to go to our rooms and do any homework or school work that was due or late.

When we got to the rooms I finished everything that I needed to do within a half hour. I was good about staying ahead in everything that I did. I helped Hailey with some of her homework since she didn't understand a lot of it and I already passed all of the classes that she was taking now. She was a junior in high school. I couldn't believe that we all would have to take an exam and pass it if we wanted to move on. It wasn't fair in my opinion. I have never had to take an exam in my life. The public school that I went to before I started online classes never took exams. We only had to take tests. The other kids never even took tests. I was going to help them the best that I could so they could be prepared and pass.

After everyone was done with their homework we all gathered downstairs for a snack before bed. I made ice cream sundaes for everyone. That was the most chaotic thing that has ever happened in that house while I was there. It all started by Allie putting whipped cream on everyone. Then of course everyone followed in her footsteps. Before Mary knew it everyone was hyper and going out of control. She had a hard time trying to get us to calm down and go up to our rooms for bed. She eventually got us all up in our rooms by nine thirty.

That night Hailey did something that she hasn't done before. She actually picked out her clothes for the next day.

"Why are you picking out clothes for tomorrow, Hailey? You never do that. You are always wait 'til the last minute to do everything."

"Yes, I know. Tomorrow is different though. Mary said that I was allowed to go to church in the morning. I found one that is just down the street from here. It was built twenty three years ago in nineteen seventy two."

"Oh, okay. What time are you leaving in the morning?"

"The church service starts at eight."

"May I come with you, Hailey? I think I want to try and go to church again. I don't have to be at work until noon tomorrow."

"It is okay with me as long as Mary gives you permission to go."

"Okay, I will ask her in the morning."

"Sounds great, Julie. I am excited for you."

"Thank you."

That night I kept thinking about what it would be like to go back to church.

The last time I was at church it was with my dad. It wasn't a good experience though. It is still a blur to me because I try not to remember the bad memories I have with my dad. I only remember some of it.

It was a cold and rainy Sunday morning. Our car broke down about a mile away from the church and we were running late. My dad decided to pick me up and run with me the rest of the way to the church. By the time we got to the church we both were soaking wet. It was nice though because I always enjoyed the rain and so I got to enjoy what I like to call my peaceful time. When we got in the church we quietly walked through the doors and sat in the back rows of the pews so no one realized that we were coming in late. We sat through the message intently. The message was intriguing.

The preacher was talking about the cross. I remember taking notes that day because my dad was. We were in the books of Joel and Jeremiah. The notes I took were these:

We shall return to the Lord with fasting, weeping and mourning. The Lord is gracious and merciful. The Lord has done marvelous things. The Lord's people will never be put to shame. (Jeremiah 24:7) Then I will give them a heart to know Me, that I am the Lord; and they shall be My people, and I will be their God, for they shall return to me with their whole heart.

As soon as I got done writing my notes something terrible happened. The church doors flew open and the police came rushing in. They pulled my dad up and said, "You are under arrest for the kidnapping of Julie." Everyone was just looking at us like we were insane. My dad tried to explain to them that it was a huge misunderstanding and that I was his daughter. Apparently, my mom made a false report to the police saying that my dad took me and told her that he wasn't going to bring me back. That wasn't true at all. I will never forget that day. That was the day that the fighting between my parents started and never stopped.

I was hoping that this church experience would be different.

Chapter 19

That next morning Hailey got me up around seven so I could get ready to go to church with her. I thought that was sweet of her to actually make sure that I woke up on time. Hailey said that Alexander usually goes to church, but since he is still recovering he couldn't go with us. He is a Christian and saved. I did have a dress that I packed with me before I left to begin this long journey of mine. It was a black and white one with flower designs on it. It used to belong to my Aunt when she was a little girl. It was my dad's sister's. Right before she died three years ago though she passed it on to me. It was in really good condition, taking into account that it was almost a hundred years old. When I put the dress on I think Hailey about fainted.

"Julie. That is such a pretty dress. I love it!"

"Thank you. It was my Aunt's."

"It looks good on you. I already asked Mary if you could come with me this morning and she said that you could. You just had to make sure that you were back and at work on time."

"I will. Let's get going. I am really excited."

"Okay, Julie. We will leave here in a minute. I just have to finish doing my hair."

"You already look perfect enough, Hailey. You don't have to spend that much time on your hair. If you spend anymore time on your hair then by the time we get to the church then the service will already be over," I laughed.

"Whatever, Julie. I am done so we can get going."

"Good."

We quietly walked out the door because everyone else was still sleeping. They usually don't get up until around nine. That is what they get for staying up so late every night. When we got to the church there were a lot of people there. I recognized only one person when we got there. That was Mr. Popas. I had no idea that he came to this church or even went to church. I ran up to him to say hi. I must have scared him because he jumped when I just gently touched his shoulder.

"Julie. What are you doing here? I didn't know that you came here."

"I could say the same exact thing to you, Mr. Popas. I came with a girl that lives in the group home with me."

I pulled Hailey beside me.

"Mr. Popas, this is Hailey. Hailey, this is Mr. Popas. He is my boss at the art studio."

Hailey didn't say a word. All she did was shrug her shoulder.

"She can be really shy at times."

"That's alright, Julie. Follow me and I will introduce you to my family."

Mr. Popas and his family were sitting right there in the front. His wife and his three stepchildren. They looked just like they did in the pictures that were in the pictures he had in his office at the studio.

"Hailey, Julie, this is my wife and three children."

"Hi. I am Julie."

They as well didn't say anything to me, but they did shake my hand. His wife pulled him aside and whispered something in his ear. I couldn't quite make out what she was telling him. I couldn't even read her lips. Reading lips were the one thing that I was actually really good at. He said something back to her but it was the same for him. I couldn't read what he was saying either. All he did was put his head down after he was done telling her what he needed to say.

"Julie. You and Hailey are welcome to sit with my family today during the service."

"Well, that is nice of you to say. I think we will just have to take you up on that offer."

By the time we sat down it was time for the service to start. One thing that Mr. Popas didn't tell me was that he was the pastor of the church. That was really interesting to me. All I wanted to know was if he was a pastor then why was he working at the art studio during the week. I was interested in what Mr. Popas was going to speak on today. Before he started giving his message we all as a church sang a couple songs. I loved singing so I really liked that part.

When we were done singing Mr. Popas started speaking. His message was on Faith. He had one statement that was the main message today. It really stuck with me. That statement was "Faith is the victory that overcomes the world, and without faith it is impossible to please God." That statement just kept running through my mind throughout the whole message. He also said that eternal life is received by grace through faith. I had no idea what that meant at the time. At the end of the message he said that point meant that you can only have eternal life if you believe in Jesus Christ and ask him to be your personal savior and if you have faith. That really got to me. After church was over I told Hailey to go home and that I would be home shortly. I just had to talk to Mr. Popas for a few minutes. So when she left I went to try and find Mr. Popas. He was by his family talking to another family.

"Mr. Popas. May I speak with you for a few minutes?"

"Sure, Julie. What is going on?"

"I was listening to your message and your very last statement made me truly think. I used to go to church with my dad when I was younger, which I enjoyed, when I went though I really didn't think about any of it. I knew that there was a God, but I really didn't have faith at the time. Now seeing how it is affecting Hailey and changing her life, I think I am ready to have faith and accept Jesus Christ as my personal savior."

"That is great news, Julie. I am glad that my message said something to you. May I pray with you?"

"Sure. I would really appreciate that, Mr. Popas."

"Dear Heavenly Father. I just come to you with Julie and her decision to accept you into her heart. I just pray that you help her come to know you more. That Hailey can just be a big encouragement to her and that they both will help each other out when it comes to them struggling. I also pray that you help Julie have faith in you in everything that she does. I just thank you Lord for bringing Julie into my life. In all this I pray in your name. Amen."

"Thank you so much, Mr. Popas."

"You are welcome, Julie. Do you have a Bible at home?"

"No, I do not."

"Would you like one?"

"I would love one, Mr. Popas."

"Great. If you just wait a few minutes and we will walk together back to my office and I will give you one."

I sat quietly waiting to go back to Mr. Popas' office to get a Bible. His family kept staring at me. I didn't like it. Didn't like it one bit. I eventually just turned my back that way I wouldn't have to see their faces. That solved a lot of situations. After about forty minutes Mr. Popas was finally done talking to other families.

I was half asleep by the time that he was ready. So instead of waking me up he just went to go get the Bible. He then came back and woke me up. I then thanked him for the

Bible and told him that I would see him in a little bit when I showed up for work. He then gave me a ride home because he didn't want me getting in an accident since I was still half asleep when he woke me up. I don't know how he knew, but he knew exactly where I lived. I thought that was odd because I was sure I never told him. Oh well, I was too tired to think. When I went inside I fell on the couch and went right to sleep.

Mary had to wake me up so I wasn't late for work. Right before I left I grabbed my Bible. I wanted to try and read it a little bit if I had any free time at work today. I didn't know what Mr. Popas was going to have me doing today. I was really hoping that he would have me on the cash register a little bit. I really enjoyed that yesterday when I did it. It seemed to come pretty easy to me. Around eleven thirty I started walking to work. I felt a lot better after I took that little nap. I had no idea why I passed out. I didn't think that I was that tired. It must have been needed though.

When I got to the store Mr. Popas was waiting for me. I was right when I said that he might have me on the cash register today. The older lady was usually the only one that did the cash register, but she wasn't even there today.

"Julie. Today I am going to have you strictly on the cash register. You will not be doing anything else today. I am expecting a lot of people to come in today and pick up their orders. I thought that today would be a good chance for you to get a lot of experience handling the customers. You will soon realize that not everybody is as nice as the one lady was the other day. I think you will do perfectly today. Remember just have faith in God and you will be able to achieve anything that you put your mind to. I see that you brought your Bible with you. You can keep it in the one drawer beneath the counter so you don't lose it or get it dirty. Then when you have any free time you will be able to read it if you like."

"Thank you so much, Mr. Popas. I am excited to start this new chapter in my life. I will do my very best to do everything that you expect me to do. I will not let you down. I can promise you that."

"Good. Now the first person that should be coming any minute now is Alan Alpe. He is an older gentleman. I will be observing you throughout the day. If you do a good job then there may be a pay raise for you here in the next month or two."

"Thank you."

The first couple of hours went pretty well if I said so myself. I did exactly what I did yesterday with the eight customers that came in. It took all the way up until my break at three to get done with everyone. It did get a little busy. That is just because there were four people that came in one after another. Since I was really the only one that was doing the cash register and getting people their orders it took me a while. I had to go to the room each time. I got it though. A lot of the people were impressed with how well I was doing. I got a couple compliments.

Some of those compliments were, "Wow, you are doing great young lady" and, "I can't believe that this is only your second day working here." All of those compliments were

143

really nice to receive. I didn't think that I would ever hear some of those words. That is just because I never thought that I could really do a good job at anything. Those are why it took me until three to get everything done.

At my break I was just about to sit down and read my Bible for a little bit when all of a sudden Hailey came running into the studio. When she got in the studio she was out of breath. She could barely talk without blowing air out. By the look on her face something was really wrong. Not just like something is broken wrong but something really bad happened and it could ruin our futures or something like that.

"What is wrong, Hailey? Is everyone alright?"

She had a hard time at first trying to speak actual words. All that came out was mumbo jumbo. I couldn't understand a single thing that she said.

"Hailey. Speak to me, what is wrong?"

"No, everything's not alright. You have to come with me right away. Alexander is back in the hospital. He all of a sudden turned pale and passed out. Mary called the ambulance again and they are on their way to the house right now. Mary told me to hurry up and come get you and see if you could possibly get off work early to come with all of us to the hospital."

I looked back at Mr. Popas. He heard everything. He didn't even think twice.

"Go, Julie. I will cover the rest of your shift. Don't you

worry about a single thing. Your family needs you more than I do right now. Just remember, keep your faith."

Hailey and I ran out of the door. I knew where the hospital was so we sprinted there. We went so fast that the people that were on the sidewalks had to watch out because we weren't slowing down or paying any attention to our surroundings.

We were greeted in the hospital lobby by Mary. She told us that we had to stay down in the lobby and that only she was allowed up Alexander at the moment. I yelled and tried to get past her. I made it to the elevator. Then a nurse finally caught me and basically dragged me back to the lobby. Hailey tried to escape as well. All of the other girls seemed a lot more calm. I couldn't believe that they could just sit there and not even try to go see Alexander. He needed us. Hailey and I both knew that. There were two guards that sat with us the whole entire time so that they made sure we didn't try and escape to the room again. I was pacing back and forth while biting my nails. One of the nurses bought all of us girls some food. Even though I was hungry there was no way that I could possibly eat. Hailey made me sit down and eat something little at least. She didn't want me to get sick or worse end up like Alexander. I agreed with her so I listened and I sat down and ate. I only ate the ham and cheese sandwich though. I then decided that I would tell Hailey that me and Alexander were boyfriend and girlfriend. I pulled her to the side.

"Hailey, I need to tell you something."

"What is it, Julie?"

"Alexander and I are boyfriend and girlfriend."

"YOU ARE WHAT?" Hailey yelled.

I quickly covered her mouth with my hand. "Shut up now, will you. Yes. The other day when Alexander came home we decided that we would take the chance and date. So that night he and I snuck out of the house and went to this one tree that I call 'our tree.' If you climb the tree you are able to see the Twin Towers. At night they are so pretty when they are all lit up. It was for sure a sight to see. Never mind that though. That is my boyfriend in there that is needing me there right beside him. Since Mary doesn't know I'm not allowed up there. I know that I am supposed to have faith just like Mr. Popas preached about this morning, but I just don't know how I can right now, Hailey. I am literally falling to pieces inside. What should I do, Hailey? I just can't and won't deal with any of this for much longer."

"First, you need to calm down. Everything will be alright. You don't see me or any of the other girls freaking out as much do you? No. That is because we all figured out that everything will be alright. Second, I think you should tell Mary about you and Alexander. It will make everything a lot more easier. Lastly, you should just keep the faith. God knows what he is doing. He always has and always will. He has a plan for everyone. Whether or not you know it yet you will figure that out eventually."

"I am trying to calm down. It is just hard for me. Next, I am not telling Mary. There is no way. If I tell her I take the risk of getting yelled at and possibly kicked out of the house. I am not ready for that. I understand that God has a plan, but right now his plan is including someone that I love. It was first taking my dad away, then my mom becoming depressed and treating me like a slave and now it is Alexander. I can't do this anymore. You know what, just leave me alone right now. I am going back to the house. I do not care what Mary says right now. There is nothing that anyone can do right now to stop me either."

"Whatever you say, Julie. Just know that if Mary asked where you went I am telling her the truth. I will not lie for you again. Especially after what you just told me. You deserve all that is coming towards you. When you get home you should pray."

"Whatever you say, Hailey. I don't know if I can truly pray right now. It will be way too difficult for me." After I said that I ran home. I didn't care anymore. Right when I got to the house I wasn't even in the front door yet when I just broke down crying. I couldn't stand all of this pain anymore. I was just wishing that God would have put the pain on me instead of the one I loved. He was the very first guy that I actually had a moment with. He is the one that has my heart. So why in the world did God have to put all the pain on him and then all of the suffering on the rest of us.

Chapter 20

When I got home I knew I was going to be the only one there for the rest of the night. I knew how to take care of myself so I didn't think there was anything that could go wrong. I had plenty of food and water for the night. That evening I was just getting out of the shower when the voice showed up again. It scared me so much I slipped on water and fell against the wall as well as bumped my head. I screamed at the top of my lungs. You would think that someone was murdering me if you heard me screaming.

"Where did you come from? Why are you here? I told you I didn't want anything to do with you last time you appeared."

"I'm so sorry, Julie. I honestly didn't mean to scare you like that. I wanted to see if you would want any help tonight around the house since you are the only physical person here."

"No! I do not want any help. Especially not from you! I don't even believe in you. I think you are just a piece of my imagination from my past that needs to leave and never bother me again. I'm seventeen years old and am an independent young lady. I have had enough of you. I am going to take my medication and hope that you will go away and things will go back to being quiet around here. Good bye and thank you very much."

"I'm not going away, Julie, no matter how much you want me to. I was sent to help you and be a guide. Since you are dating Alexander I have to give guidance to you. I will always be here. I won't say another word to you unless you speak first. You don't have to worry about me. Have a great night, Julie."

After that conversation I did everything in my power to block out the voice. I knew that it was all in my head. My medication helped my brain that night. When I finally did fall asleep I had a peaceful dream.

I was older, married to someone that wasn't Alexander and had three kids. We were all on the beach playing in the water. A photographer that was there offered to take our family photo so she could get some practice in. It was a nice time. It started to storm in my dream. That is when I woke up. I didn't want the dream to end. It was so perfect.

When I woke up it was only eight at night. I wasn't tired enough to go back to bed. I decided I would get up and clean the house for the week. I didn't know how long Alexander and everyone else would be at the hospital and the house needed to be cleaned no matter what the circumstances were. When I went downstairs I put some music on so I could focus more.

I was about to head down to the basement to get some laundry started. When I opened the door before I stepped down there was a basket full of clothes already done and folded. I didn't remember anyone else doing the laundry before all of the craziness started to happen. Maybe while I was at work or something someone did it for me. All I know is that the laundry is my chore to do at least once a week. I would do it more if it was necessary. I then took the basket and put all the clothes away. When I finally did make it down to the basement there were even more baskets of clothes done and folded. I knew something was going on, but I couldn't quite put my finger on what it was. That was almost all of the laundry. I couldn't believe it. I have never been able to get all of the laundry done in one day. I didn't know what or why things were happening. Half of me was thinking that the voice was real and was truly in my life to help me out with coping with different situations in my life. I kept thinking it over and was trying to determine if I was going to give this voice a chance to try and help me. I knew it was crazy because I knew it was all part of my imagination.

"Are you there?" There was nothing but silence. "Listen, I know you are here. I want to apologize for my stubbornness and for me not believing in you. I thought you were all in my mind. I thought I was going crazy like my mother. When I finally got some help that I needed you never appeared again. At that point I figured out that the possibility of you being part of my mind playing games on me was prominent. After you showed up again while talking to Alexander I knew or at least thought I knew that you were part of his imagination. Now you show up just when I need help. I now know that you have always been here to help Alexander and I."

"Yes, I have, Julie. I never wanted anything but to be a guide for you. I will always be around no matter what. All you will have to do it call out to me and I will be there to help with anything you may need."

"Thank you. I have one more question for you, were you the one that helped me with all of the laundry?"

"No. I am part of your imagination. I can't do anything physically. Mary did it when you left to go find Alexander."

"Thank you. I appreciate everything. I don't know what I would do without your help."

"It's no problem. Now go back to bed and when you get up you can enjoy the rest of your day."

"Thank you. I think I might just do that."

After all of the cleaning was done it was only nine. I wanted to be back at the hospital with everyone. I called Mary and she came to pick me up and she took me back to the hospital to be with everyone else. When I got up to see Alexander he was sleeping and he was the only one on my mind for the rest of the evening. By eleven o'clock that night I finally broke down crying. I threw myself on the couch that was in the hospital room and just let it all out. I finally gathered myself together and wanted to get away for a little bit.

I went back to the lobby to try and get some rest, but before I fell asleep I got a surprise visit. I couldn't believe who it was.

Chapter 21

It was Mr. Popas. I guess Mary got a hold of him because she didn't think that it was best for me to be around when we weren't sure what was wrong with Alexander, because she knew how attached I was to him and how close we were. All I could was break down crying again. Mr. Popas gave me a hug and came in and sat on the couch beside me.

"What is going on, Julie?"

"Alexander is in really bad shape. I hate seeing him like this. I like him so much. He is the first one that has helped me on my journey. I feel like he was the first one that I completely trusted. I don't understand why God is doing this. He first took my dad away and now he is putting Alexander through all of this pain. I just want all of this to go away."

"I totally understand how you are feeling, Julie. I am here for you, as well as God is always there for you. I would like you to grab your Bible and turn to 1 Peter 5:10. This is a verse that I really enjoy to read when I am down."

"Okay."

I grabbed my Bible and turned to where Mr. Popas told me to.

"Will you read to me, Julie, what that verse says."

I read it out loud to him, "But the God of all grace, who hath called us unto his eternal glory by Christ Jesus, after that ye have suffered a while, make you perfect, establish, strengthen, settle you."

"Good job, Julie. Now just keep that verse in mind while you are going through this rough time. God knows what he is doing. He always has and always will. Mary called me because she didn't think it would be best for you to stay here and so I talked it over with my family and they would love to have you stay if that is something that you would be interested in doing."

"I'm not sure about that, Mr. Popas. I had a feeling that earlier today when we were at church your family didn't like me that."

"Julie. That is not true. My wife thinks that you are really sweet and amazing. She was the first one that actually offered for you to stay with us overnight while Mary and everyone else is at the hospital. I just agreed with her that it would be a great idea. Also I think you would get along with my children a lot. They are just like you in some ways."

"Okay, Mr. Popas. I will take you up on your offer then and stay with you and your family tonight. Can we agree on one thing though?"

"What would that be, Julie?"

"That if I get scared or don't want to stay there the whole night then you will take me back to the hospital so I can be with everyone."

"Okay, Julie. I will agree with you on that."

"Thank you."

We drove back to my house, and I went upstairs to pack my pajamas and an outfit for tomorrow. I had to grab my laptop so I could still do my school work no matter where I was. I needed to make sure that I didn't get behind just because of family situations that were going on. As soon as I got all packed up and everything we headed to Mr. Popas' house. Surprisingly he only lived about five minutes away from the studio and my house. It was a very nice house. It was just a plain brick house, but he had a very nice garden in his front yard.

"My wife loves to garden. She has kept a garden for the past five years. The children love helping her out with it. For me I am not a garden person at all. Flowers and that stuff just never really interested. Even when I was younger they never did."

After he said that he reminded me of someone that I knew. I just couldn't quite put my finger on who it was that I was thinking of. When I got inside Mr. Popas showed me where I would be sleeping. They had a guest room that I would be using. It wasn't very big, but it was big enough for me. It had a blue wallpaper with gray stripes on all four walls. The walls kind of reminded me of like a big present in some way.

"Thank you, Mr. Popas, for letting me stay here tonight."

"You are welcome, Julie. I will let you get settled in and I will come and get you when it is time for dinner. We are having barbecue chicken and vegetables."

154

"Thanks."

While I was getting settled in one of the girls came in my room. I tried to make conversation with her. When I tried to say hi though she just stood there and just stared at me. It was getting really awkward between us.

"What are you doing just standing there? It is getting really awkward and rude. What is your name?"

She still didn't say anything. I was starting to get frustrated with her. I went down to ask Mr. Popas why she wouldn't talk to me.

"Mr. Popas. One of your daughters won't talk to me. She just stood at my door and stared at me. Why is that?"

"Oh, Julie. I forgot to tell you that Sophia is deaf. You can only communicate to her through sign language. She wasn't trying to be rude at all. She just didn't hear you. She has been this way for the past two years. We as a family had a terrible accident. We were in a bad car accident. We did make it out of the car before something terrible happened. As soon as we got out of the car it blew up in flames. We were far enough away from the car except for Sophia. She was still close enough to the explosion to where it blew her ear drums out. The explosion is what caused her to become deaf. We all had to take sign language classes so we could still communicate with Sophia. "

"I am so sorry to hear about the bad car accident. I had no idea. My apologies. The accident makes a lot more sense though. Thank you for clearing that up for me."

When I knew that I figured out a perfect way to communicate with Sophia. I did not know sign language, but since she knew how to read and write I was assuming I would just use paper and marker to communicate with her, or something else.

I took out my laptop and opened a Word document. I typed a little and then she responded. This is what she told me in her response:

My name is Sophia. I am thirteen years old. I am not really that happy that you are staying the night with us so I will just let you know that right from the beginning. Ever since my dad told us all about you I haven't liked you. My dad will never love you as much as he loves my siblings and I. I would rather you not try to talk to at least me while you are staying here. My siblings may feel differently about you, but my feelings will never change. I have told you everything that I wanted to tell you. So I hope you have a great night. Also so you know I can not wait til you go back with your family tomorrow.

When I read that I felt so many different things at the same exact time. First, I felt confused. I didn't know what she meant by when she said that he will never love me as much as he loved them. I knew he would never love me as much as he did them because I wasn't his child. I was so frustrated because I missed my dad and the statement just made it a lot more hurtful. They were his children and nothing would ever change that. I had no control over anything. It seemed like she thought that I did. Lastly, I felt like I wanted to cry. Sophia hurt my feelings so badly. How could she be so mean to me? She was such a bully. I have never been so hurt in my entire life. Her dad was a pastor and I would think that she would be raised a lot better than to be mean to people. When I first met her I thought she was this nice, sweet and quiet girl who really didn't talk much. I wasn't trying to come in between her or her family. Mr. Popas was just trying to help me while I was going through a rough time right now. If she wanted to be like that then I was going to let her. I would just play along with her little act.

When I went down for dinner it was pretty silent between everyone. I didn't have that much to say to anyone down there. Especially Sophia. Sophia did exchange some looks with me though. They weren't good ones at all. I was getting really upset. I think Mr. Popas could tell because after dinner he pulled me aside.

"Are you okay, Julie? You were quiet at dinner and you didn't eat that much either."

"To be honest I am not okay."

"Why is that, Julie?"

"Sophia said some pretty mean and upsetting things to me. I didn't like what she said. Not one bit."

"May I see what she said to you if you have it in physical form."

"I do."

I handed him my laptop and opened the Word document. After he read it I could tell that he was shocked. He said he knew that it was Sophia that said it because in her response she told me how old she was and Mr. Popas never told me how old any of his children were. He told me that he would sit Sophia down and try to figure out why she said all of this to me. He knew sign language so he could communicate to her better than I could.

So after a little while Mr. Popas went upstairs to try and talk to Sophia. I was told to stay downstairs until bedtime. That way Sophia didn't get any more upset than she already was going to be. Mr. Popas said that when she got into trouble by anyone then she would have a huge fit and throw herself on the ground, as well as she will start throwing stuff everywhere in her room. He said he was looking out for us both when he said it was best for me to just stay downstairs.

I am kind of glad that he did tell me to not come anywhere near Sophia at the time. I could hear that things were not going the way that she expected. I started to hear things bang everywhere. I think I might have even heard something break. It sounded like it was glass. When Mr. Popas came downstairs he got into a drawer and got a lock out of one of the junk drawers, the one drawer that had all of the sharp supplies and kitchen utensils in. Apparently when Sophia got in these moods and had episodes like this she was locked inside of her room so she couldn't come down and hurt anyone. To be honest I truly think that it was a good idea that Sophia was locked in her room.

"I'm so sorry that you have to experience all of this, Julie. I will understand if you don't want to stay here and want to go back to the hospital with everyone."

"No, it is okay, Mr. Popas. I understand how she feels."

"Okay. I told her that she has to write an apology note to you before the end of tonight. What she did was wrong and not right. It was uncalled for. I have no clue what has gotten into her. She has never acted this way towards anyone before. It is so strange."

"It is okay, Mr. Popas, I understand. She just doesn't want anyone new in her life. That is how I was when I first moved in with Mary and everyone. Then eventually I warmed up to everyone and they all accepted me for me. I was appreciative about that. It will just take her some time. Just trust me on this one, Mr. Popas."

"Okay, I trust you, Julie. I always will. I knew from the moment you walked into the art studio that you were going to be trustworthy."

"Thank you. That means a lot to me."

I waited a little while longer to go upstairs just in case Sophia found some way to get out of her room. I truly doubt that she could because by the looks of it the lock that Mr. Popas took out of the drawer looked like it would be impossible for her to break out of her room. When I went back up into the guest room there on the bed laid a note. It was decorated all pretty on the outside of it too. This is what the note said:

Julie. I am so sorry about the way that I acted earlier. I have no idea what got into me. This is not my typical behavior. I can promise you that. I guess I just got a little jealous about you staying here overnight. I didn't see the true reason behind it to be completely honest with you. Now I see that my dad was just trying to help you. He really does care a lot about you. There is another reason behind that, but I am not allowed telling you that reason. You will find that out at a later time. Again, I am truly sorry for my actions. I did not mean to hurt your feelings. I am glad that you are staying with us. I hope you can find in your heart a reason to forgive me. Thank you.

Sincerely,

Sophia.

That note about made me tear up. I couldn't believe her. After that I had no choice but to forgive Sophia. That was the least I could do. I wrote a note back to Sophia before I went back to bed. This is what my response was back to Sophia:

Hey Sophia.

I am going to apologize now for the long length of my response. Here it goes. I appreciate that you apologized to me. It means a lot to me. It shows me that you are a strong and independent young lady. I know that you are truly sorry for your actions. I can understand how you are feeling. I know that you are just not wanting to get used to someone being in your life and then leaving you. I have had that done to me before. My dad when I was fifteen years old he left my mom and I. That hurt me a lot. I didn't know why he left and didn't take me with him. I really wish that he would have. If he did I don't think I would be here right now. The only good thing about me not being with him right now is that I wouldn't of probably met you. Now I don't know that for a fact, but I just wouldn't know. Your dad may care about me, but he definitely cares about you and your family a lot more. I can tell because he has a lot of photos of you guys in his office at the art studio. So if you ever feel like your dad doesn't care about you then just go to the art studio and go check his office. Then you will know what I mean. You may have hurt my feelings a little earlier, but you have definitely made up for that. Your apology note was really nice of you. The design on the outside was absolutely amazing. I can't believe that you drew all of it. It was really good. You should try and get a job at the studio when you get older. You would be really good at that. Thank you again. I accept your apology.

Sincerely,

Julie.

I slipped it under the door. It sounded like she was asleep because there was no noise on the other side. I knew that she would get it in the morning.

Chapter 22

When I got woken up it was not pleasant. It was by Mr. Popas violently shaking me telling me that I needed to get up and that we needed to get to the hospital right away. I didn't have any time to have any breakfast and I was starving. I just wished that I could go back to sleep. I was sleeping so peacefully. Mr. Popas made sure that I took my medicine last night before bed so I could actually sleep well. I wanted all of this to stop. I wanted to wake up and do what I usually do in the morning with my loving new family at Mary's. I was so used to my routine by now that anything different like this morning was going to ruin everything. I did not like it one bit.

It would be different if someone told me what was happening and why we needed to hurry up to get to the hospital. The thought of the hospital just made me sick. I didn't want to be there knowing that I couldn't control myself since Alexander was sick. No matter how many times I would ask Mr. Popas to tell what in the world was going on he wouldn't tell me what was going on or why we needed to get to the hospital. I was getting frustrated with him. I did decide to listen to him though and quickly got up and get ready.

Before I left the house Sophia gave me another letter back. She told me not to open it though until I got to the hospital. I agreed that I wouldn't open it 'til I was at the hospital. I really wanted to open the letter beforehand though. Again it was all decorated so pretty and fancy. This girl had some serious talent whether or not she would admit she did or not.

Mr. Popas drove as fast as he could to get to the hospital. He said we needed to get there before something really bad happened. He also reassured me that whatever happened to not worry and that God is in control of everything. That statement made me worry even more. I couldn't even think about all of the possibilities of things that could be wrong. Was Alexander worse than what he was yesterday? Did someone else get sick or what happened? I wanted answers, but no one would give me the answers that I wanted. I was so stressed out over everything. I really wish I could have talked to my therapist. That is the one person that I really wanted at that moment. I knew I had to wait another week until I saw her though. I just had to keep going with the flow.

When we got to the hospital I found all of the other girls in the hospital lobby crying. Automatically I knew that whatever happened or was about to happen was to the point where they just couldn't handle it anymore. I tried asking them what the heck was going on, but no one would answer me they just sat there crying. I felt hopeless because since I didn't know what was going on, I couldn't help them as much as I wanted to. It was so sad. Then when I saw Mary come down from Alexander's room she was crying as well, but at least she sat me down and told me what was going on.

"Julie. Listen to me. You are not going to like hearing what I am about to say, but it needs to be said. Alexander is in really bad condition. Last time we came here with Alexander doctors promised us that everything was going to be alright. They didn't think that anything would happen to Alexander. Well now that he is back in here they did some more tests. This time in the tests they found something really bad. The thing that they found was that he has something called Sepsis. Sepsis is when bacteria enters the bloodstream. It can cause blood poisoning. If untreated then it can become life threatening. Since we didn't know that Alexander had it until this morning then the doctors are thinking that it may be too late. They are doing everything they can to treat it quickly. Now they are saying that they don't think that he will make it until the end of the day. I am so sorry Julie. I know he meant a lot to you. Hailey told me about you two. I am totally fine with you and Alexander being together. I thought that I should have told you before any of the girls told you."

After Mary said that I didn't know what to say or think. I just couldn't believe any of this. I did break down and cry. I wanted all of this to just be a dream. I wanted to wake up and all of this not be true and everything to just go back to normal. I knew that the chances of any of that happening was slim to nothing. As soon as it all settled in as reality I ran all the way up to Alexander's hospital room. No one tried to stop me either. All I wanted was to be there right beside him. He needed me more then anything right now. I just knew he did, even if he couldn't think properly or even know that I was up in that room with him. I wanted to be with my boyfriend. Nothing and no one would stop me either.

When I got there I suddenly stopped right at his door. I wanted to think for a minute about what I was about to do. The room that I was about to enter had the one person that wasn't going to be in my life anymore after today. Right before I entered the room I took a deep breath. I walked to his bedside and knelt on my knees so I could pray.

"Dear Heavenly Father, I come to you to pray for Alexander. I just pray that you help him through all of this pain that he is going through. I know that you have a plan for him. He has done great things. He has been an amazing friend to me. He has also been a great boyfriend to me in the past couple of days. I just pray that you help him and help all of his family while we are going through this rough time. I thank you again for everything. Even the pain and suffering. I couldn't imagine my life without you in it now. I'm glad that you have showed me your love. I am glad that you showed me the way to have faith in you. In all this I pray in Jesus name. Amen."

As soon as I was done praying Mr. Popas came in and hugged me.

"I am so proud of you, Julie, for praying to God and just giving all of your troubles to him. You have grown to be a great young lady."

"Thank you, Mr. Popas, for everything."

"You are welcome, Julie."

I then still had the last letter that Sophia has given me. I opened it and this is what she had to told me.

Julie.

Thank you for accepting my apology. I hope that we can be great friends. I don't know if when you are reading this if my dad has told you the great news yet or not, but all I have to say is welcome to the crazy, loving and welcoming family. Also, thank you for all of your compliments that you gave me. They all meant a lot to me. I am self conscious about myself. I don't get many compliments that much. I was considering working with my dad when I am old enough. My dad said that I have to wait til I am fifteen years old. I do help my dad a little already by designing some of the paintings that are in the studio. I only do those in my free time though. I also painted the guest room five years ago when we all moved in the house. It took me about a month to finish the whole room. I am glad that you liked the room. I hope that you can stay with us a lot more. I will admit that you are a pretty cool girl. You are amazing and unique. I heard that yesterday after church you accepted Jesus Christ as your personal Savior. That right there is something that makes you special. You are now a child of God. Nothing and no one can take that away from you. I am especially happy that my dad could be there for your special moment. I hope you always know that I am here for you. I am just a text away. Thank you again. Love you.

Love,

Sophia

When I read that I shed a tear or two. They were good tears though. I was so happy that Sophia felt the way that she told me in her letter. The only thing I still do not know is why Mr. Popas was still hiding something from me. Everyone in his family knew something that I didn't. I really wish I would know what everyone else knows. I was about to ask him, but when I turned around he wasn't there anymore. I thought he was right behind me, but I guess I was wrong. I knew he

166

would be back in the room soon. Before he came in I wanted to talk to Alexander about everything.

"Hey, Alexander. I know this is rough, but I know you will get through this."

Alexander could barely talk because he was so out of breath but he managed to say, "Thank you, Julie. I don't know how much longer I can fight this."

"Don't fight it, Alexander. It is causing so much more pain for you."

"If I stop fighting I'll lose you and I don't want to lose you."

"It's okay, Alexander. I'll be fine. I want you to be in peace."

"Okay Julie. I think I'm going to take another nap."

"Okay, Alexander." I gave him a quick kiss on the cheek. I decided that I would just take another quick nap too. I had another amazing dream.

This dream was about when my dad was still around and in my life when I was a little girl. I remembered that every first Wednesday of each month my dad would take me out to dinner at a restaurant of my choice. I always chose this little restaurant called "Lenny's." They had the most amazing pasta that I would chose every single time that we went. I would eat it all and then I would complain that my stomach hurt. After dinner, even though I was full, we would always go to the park and walk around. We would also stop at an ice cream truck every single time. The only exception would be if it was the winter time instead of ice cream we would get hot chocolate. The hot chocolate was really good. My friends mom owned that ice cream truck. She would often give us discounts since we were close friends. I really liked when she would do that. Then after that we would go home to my mom and finish the night by playing a couple of board games and then finally watch my favorite movie "Teenage Mutant Ninja Turtles." I loved that movie and I still do. My dream kept and was being so peaceful and relaxing. When I woke up Mr. Popas was back in the room.

There was a present at my feet.

"What is this for?"

"It is just a little present for you to show you how much I appreciate you dealing with Sophia last night and accepting her apologies. I saw the letter that you wrote her back. I thought that was pretty amazing. It really showed that you have an amazing attitude towards everything. You are so sweet, caring, loving, kind and last but not least you are unique in your very own way. I couldn't of asked for anyone better than you. You are such a great role model to everyone around you. So to show you thank you I got you a little something."

"You didn't have to though, Mr. Popas. I was just being me."

"I know I didn't have to, but I wanted to."

"Well, thank you."

I carefully picked up the little box and opened it. When I opened it inside was a really pretty dress. It was long and red. Then right underneath the dress there was a necklace and a bracelet. On the bracelet there was a Bible verse:

For God so loved the world that he gave his only begotten Son for whosoever should believeth in him shall not perish but have everlasting life. John 3:16

"That is another one of my favorite verses, Julie. It is a very known verse to everyone as well. Even if people didn't read the Bible they know this verse. I hope it will guide you in life just like it has guided me through everything."

"It is amazing, Mr. Popas. Thank you so much. This is all just great."

The necklace was a cross shaped. I knew from that moment on then whenever I felt down and needed a pick me up I could always look at the cross and remember that God is in control. He always was and always will be.

Right after I was done talking with Mr. Popas everyone else came in. Right in good timing too. Alexander's monitor went off. We all knew what that meant. We didn't want to think about what it meant but deep down inside we truly did know what it meant. It meant that we no longer had someone we cared about. We knew that God took him to a better place. God knows what he was doing though. It went completely quiet for a while. No one said a word. We sat there with grief in our eyes. We knew that nothing would be the same without Alexander around. Whether we wanted to admit it or not he made our lives at the house more adventurous. We never knew what to expect from him on a day to day basis. In my eyes everything that happened with him in the past couple of days made us come closer together as a family.

Right before Mr. Popas left so we could all just take time he gave me one last letter, but this one was a big shocker.

Julie. What I am about to tell you is something that you may not believe, but I can tell you that it is true. I am your dad. The reason I didn't try to come back is because your mom sent me messages that if I tried to come and visit you she would call the police and press charges of harassment and get a protection order against me. I had too much to lose at that time. I knew you were a strong girl and could take care of yourself. I also knew that you would eventually find me one way or another and that you did. I changed my last name when I got married again. I also grew a beard that way people wouldn't recognize me. I changed my name completely because if I wanted to start a new life that meant to have a name that no one knew me by. I have changed in the way I look in the past two years. I am sorry that I didn't tell you earlier. I really wanted to, but thought that I would keep it a secret until I knew you were ready. I will always be here for you no matter what. I hope to be part of your life now. I am sorry that I left you and your mother two years ago. I just felt like it was the best idea for everyone involved. I hope you can understand. Thank you. I love you.

Love,

Dad

That was something else. When I got that news I knew that my life was about to change. I didn't know if it was going to be for better or worse, but I was excited to find out.

Acknowledgments

This book is one that you will want to follow. Here are some of the special people that have helped me through this process. I love everyone that helped make this book become a reality.

Bob Scott Publishing - Thank you for helping me make my dream of becoming an author come true.

Erica Alexander - Thank you for helping me figure out the amazing cover.

Jodi Lea Stewart - Thank you for helping me understand the writing process and being a great encouragement to me while writing this even though I got frustrated at times.

My family and friends - Thank you for being one of my greatest support that there is.

About the Author

Skylar Hill is an ordinary young lady who has gone through similar struggles that most might not see that she has gone through. She writes in her free time has a way to express her feelings. Skylar will always continue to write whether that be short stories, novellas, children's stories, or novels. She loves traveling and helping those around her. When an opportunity comes up to travel and explore she takes the chance no matter if there is a risk involved. She considers everyone feelings but in the end she does what she wants because she only has to please God and herself. She is a Christian and tries her best to incorporate Christianity into her writing whenever possible.

Also available from Bob Scott Publishing

The Redemption of Soul Dallas
Cara Jordan White

Eighteen and homeless, Soul Dallas has more to worry about than what he'll be doing this New Year's. In a town where compassion is rare and malice plenty, he's left for dead by a gang seeking revenge for his father's debts.

When anxiety-burdened Lana provides him with shelter, she's swept into his world of pandemonium where fear means fight not flight. Leaving behind her imprisoned life with an over-bearing mother, she learns of Soul's shocking past and what it truly means to be alive. But when the gang closes ranks and Soul falls ill, finding a bright future seems futile.

Together Soul and Lana must seek reason behind an ally's betrayal, a dead woman's return, and the ruthlessness behind some people's need for vengeance.

But the pair don't always see eye to eye, and each have plans that could jepordise everything.